Only 25 Minutes from Broadway

An Anecdotal History of the Westchester Broadway Theatre

Gary D. Chattman

Strategic Book Publishing and Rights Co.

Strategic Book Publishing and Rights Co., LLC
USA | Singapore
www.sbpra.net

For information about special discounts for bulk purchases, please
contact Strategic Book Publishing and Rights Co. Special Sales, at
bookorder@sbpra.net.

ISBN: 978-1-68235-379-0

Book Design: Suzanne Kelly

Note: This book originally was written in 2016 to 2017

ORIGINAL DEDICATION

Usually with a book like this—about one of the most important contributions to American culture—Westchester Broadway Theatre, né An Evening Dinner Theatre, it is incumbent upon the author to dedicate it to someone close to him/her or to dedicate it to a muse.

I dedicate this book to the strength and courage of Von Ann and Bill Stutler and to the perseverance of Bob Funking, the co-owning producers of Westchester Broadway Theatre and to their belief that a dream which they had—the dinner theatre idea—can become realized if you have the determination and caring to believe in that dream.

Personally, I dedicate this to my wife of over forty-five years—my confidant, my love, my own muse, my spirit.

DEDICATION Written in 2020

Obviously, in retrospect, this book must be dedicated to Bill Stutler, Bob Funking, and Von Ann Stutler—and to all those thespians, crew, and staff who worked and lived at An Evening Dinner Theatre and then the Westchester Broadway Theatre (WBT), and to the many, many people who enjoyed live theatre—wonderful live theatre—only twenty-five minutes from Broadway. *Before the dream exploded because of the Coronavirus.*

We will all miss our theatre.

"What if everything goes wrong, what if sorrow comes along? Hide your feelings from the throne . . . Life can't always be a song . . . and when it's all over, the curtain, the curtain comes down." Diana Krall

"Life is a play that does not allow testing. So, sing, cry, dance, laugh and live intensely, before the curtain closes and the piece ends with no applause." Charlie Chaplin

"For many of us, the curtain has just come down on childhood." Mitch Albom

OVERTURE

"Climb ev'ry mountain, search high and low. Follow ev'ry byway, ev'ry path you know. Climb ev'ry mountain, ford ev'ry stream. Follow ev'ry rainbow, till you find your dream! A dream that will need, all the love you can give. Ev'ry day of your life for as long as you live. Climb rv'ry mountain, ford ev'ry stream. Follow ev'ry rainbow till you find your dream!" *The Sound of Music:* **Richard Rodgers and Oscar Hammerstein II**

"This is the moment, this is the day, when I send all my doubts and demons away. Ev'ry endeavour I have made ever is coming into play, is here and now today. *Jekyll and Hyde: L*eslie Bricusse and Frank Wildhorn

"The sun will come out, tomorrow. Bet your bottom dollar that tomorrow . . . there'll be sun. Jus' thinking about tomorrow, clears away the cobwebs and the sorrow till there's none." *Annie: Martin Charnin,* **Charles Strouse**

The year is 1974. Richard Nixon resigned; Gerald Ford became president; Muhammed Ali was stripped of his boxing crown for refusing the draft; inflation spiked; the 55 mph limit was imposed throughout the country on highways to save fuel; Stephen King's fourth novel but his first to be published, *Carrie,* grabbed readers; the Soviet Salyut Space Station was launched; gas shortages; Ed Sullivan died; Patty Hearst was abducted; there were Watergate hearings; *The Taking of Pelham 123* was in theatres, and Hank Aaron broke Babe Ruth's all-time home-run record.

July 1974. On the 19th, the Soviet space explorer *Soyus* landed; July llth, the House Judiciary Committee released its Watergate evidence; On July 14th, Billy Martin, manager of the Yankees, was ejected twice from two games by umpires, and on the 27th of July that year, the House Judiciary Committee voted 27–11 for the impeachment of President Nixon, and in Elmsford, New York, An Evening Dinner Theatre was born. It was Sunday, and it was hot.

So was this concept—patrons eat lunch or dinner and watch a re-creation of a wonderful Broadway show—all at a very nominal charge. And free parking! And thus was born the Evening Dinner Theatre in Elmsford (notice the "re" in theater).

It is now November 2016. It's been a long, long time, from July 1974 to November 2016. An Evening Dinner Theatre morphed into Westchester Broadway Theatre, and it's still humming, still rockin', and still entertaining thousands of people in this metropolitan area.

The dream that Bob Funking and Bill and Von Ann Stutler had in the early '70s has borne the fruit of many decades. Lunch, dinner, and a Broadway-quality show, plus parking, all for one fee that is *way* below that of Broadway—that dream is still not an impossible dream but a tradition for audiences in our tri-state area. WBT is also a cabaret that has featured such luminaries as Jackie Mason, Tom Jones, George Carlin, Paul Anka, Wayne Newton, Harry Belafonte, The New York Tenors, *Forever Motown, Simply Diamond, Beatlemania Now* . . . this theatre exemplifies the idea of "What I Did for Love"—the love of theatre by the Stutlers and Funking.

It's hard to believe that Bob Funking is eighty-three and Bill Stutler is seventy-seven. Both today are vibrant people with astonishing memories. The love of theatre will do that to you!

"If I Were a Rich Man" I'd buy $165 tickets to a Broadway show, then pay $100 for dinner and $40 for parking. But, since

I live in Westchester (only twenty-five minutes from Broadway), or Connecticut, or New Jersey, or anywhere, I can see that WBT is "All for the Best." As I put "A Spoonful of Sugar" in my coffee, after having eaten a delicious roast beef platter, having viewed a masterful Broadway musical production, with my "Mamma Mia" or my wife, or my girlfriend, or my family, I know I'm not "Far From the Home I Love"; I know that WBT provides me with "A Lot of Livin' To Do" and the enjoyment of a Broadway, Equity cast, talented creative staff, with directors like Rob Ashford, Kathleen Marshall, Susan Stroman, Charles Repole, Rob Marshall, choreographer Tommie Walsh—all who began at the Westchester Broadway Theatre/An Evening Dinner Theatre.

Stutler and Funking do more shows in one year than some producers do in a whole lifetime! *Saturday Night Fever* is their 198th production. Can you believe that?

So, ladies and gentlemen, sit back in your comfortable swivel seats. Push aside your finished, delicious dinner with its scrumptious peach melba dessert, as the house lights dim on this special thrust stage, and watch how a successful theatrical enterprise was created in Elmsford, New York, by two young advertising managers who had a dream. A miraculous dream. A dream only twenty-five minutes from Broadway: "Whisper of how I'm yearning, To mingle with the old-time throng. Give my regards to old Broadway, And say that I'll be there e'er long." (Thank you, Mr. George M. Cohan)

And "Consider Yourself" lucky to be a spectator on the "hows" and the "wheres" and the "whys" of this Westchester Broadway Theatre—An Evening Dinner Theatre. "Miracle of Miracles," created "With a Little Bit of Luck" by Bill Stutler and Bob Funking. This is a tribute to these producers—who have produced a family environment out of a business— and have inspired, nurtured, and created a glorious theatrical world—where every soul who passes through their portals knows "There's No Business Like Show Business!"

The house lights grow dimmer as we hear . . .

3

ACT I
AN EVENING DINNER THEATRE

SCENE ONE: "WE CAN DO IT!"

"*I wanna be a producer, with a hit show on Broadway. I wanna be a producer, lunch at Sardi's every day. I wanna be a producer, sport a top hat and a cane. I wanna be a producer, and drive those chorus girls insane! I'm gonna be a producer, sound the horn and beat the drum. I'm gonna be a producer, look out Broadway, here I come!.. . . What do I say, finally a chance to be a Broadway producer, what do I say? Finally a chance to make my dreams come true.*" *The Producers*: Mel Brooks and Thomas Meehan; directed by Susan Stroman (another alumnus from An Evening Dinner Theatre).

Let's set this scene: It's New York City. It's the beginning of the 1970s, inflation, stagnation. The country was in economic woe. Isn't it a perfect time for two enterprising young men to open up a dinner theatre?

Huh?

Bob Funking, a native New Yorker, was working in an ad agency named Kelly Naison in Manhattan, way after college (CCNY), and he was an account executive.

Surprise! Bill Stutler (originally from Huntington, West Virginia—he called himself a hillbilly—graduate of Michigan State University) was working there. They had a mutual friend from another agency, Jack Silverman, and Bob needed a job. He called Bill.

"Unhappy . . . unhappy . . . very, very, very unhappy"
The Producers

Jack Silverman—that mutual friend—called Bill Stutler about Bob Funking. Both future producers were then working at different agencies. The agency where Bill worked was hiring, so Bob went to be interviewed. Bob was told that there were

7

not going to be any hires. So Bob went down the hall, where there was hiring going on. Bob was then hired by the president of the company to work on the Scott Paper and Arm & Hammer accounts, and others, as a copywriter.

Their paths separated a bit, even though now they worked at the same firm . . . then . . . they got to know each other! Surprise! Karma! Lunch a couple of times began a special friendship. This agency they both worked at had very large accounts. It was that kind of an agency! (Remember baking soda in refrigerators? That was them!) So they became friends.

Bob Funking took acting classes at night during his twenties and thirties. He even took singing lessons! Unfortunately, his teacher died! He decided singing wasn't a career for him. He was also a gourmet cook. A jack of all trades—master of most!

Bill Stutler had gone to college on a drum major scholarship. He led the band and twirled the baton. Obviously, the best training for a theatrical producer! He worked at an ad agency in Chicago, then he came to New York.

So let's set the scene: A restaurant in New York. Lunch. A made-up conversation.. . . but it could have been true . . .

Bob: So, Bill, what's happening? What are you doing lately?

Bill: Oh, nothing. Have you heard about dinner theatres?

Bob: No, what?

Bill: You know. You eat a meal, then you watch a quality show.

Bob: Not like Broadway? You just pay to see a show . . .

Bill: No. Not at all. Broadway is Broadway. It's expensive. For a Broadway show, you have to have a lot of investors. The public comes in, watches a show—pays a lot of money. They also have to pay for parking. It's expensive!

Bob: I understand. So?

Bill: Well, I recently went home to visit my parents.

Bob: And . . .

Bill: They took my wife and me to a dinner theatre that was between Charleston and Huntington, West Virginia. It is called the Mountaineer Dinner Theatre. It's a brand-new thing!

Bob: Sounds interesting. I always liked theatre. I'm kinda bored doing what I'm doing.

Bill: Me, too. I have an idea.

Bob: Yes?

Bill: You know that my wife, Von Ann, and I were looking for something we could do together.

Bob: Go on. I know your wife is in the real estate business. Wasn't she also a social worker?

Bill: Yes, that's correct. I'm really fascinated about the idea. What do you think about that idea?

Bob: Sounds interesting. Why don't we check it out?

"Where is the life that late I led? Where is it now? Totally dead! *Kiss Me, Kate*: **Cole Porter**

Dinner theatres were becoming the rage around the country about 1972. So Messieurs Funking and Von Ann and Bill Stutler took a tour of dinner theatres. They went to the Chateau Deville in Warehouse Point, Connecticut, all over the place. Both men worked full-time on their advertising jobs! And Von Ann did, too! They worked on this special idea on weekends and late at night. Dedicated individuals, Bob Funking and Von Ann and Bill Stutler. They had little money—but they had this idea—and they had youth. And, as you know, when you're young, you've got lots and lots of energy and spunk and . . .

Meantime, while they were investigating dinner theatres around the country, Bill Stutler, then currently of Thornwood, New York, saw this Executive Park in Elmsford. It was being developed—adding buildings. Both Bill and Bob needed a place where all the streets would meet—easy access. *Parfait!*

Here's the scene: Two ad executives at a successful New York City agency were looking to give up their well-paying jobs to build a dinner theatre in Elmsford, New York. Yup, that's correct. You might say, why? But when you have the spark to create, especially in the theatre, you have to act. You have to. Even though they had no money, they did have a dream! ("Maybe it was a nightmare!"—Bill Stutler said.) Von Ann and Bill eventu-

9

ally would have three young kids—and two foster kids—as this business was getting off the ground.

"Where is the fun I used to find? Where has it gone? Gone with the wind." *Kiss Me, Kate*: **Cole Porter**

It usually takes two to tango, but in this case it took three. You have to have extreme energy and drive to embark on such a course. And you need as many hands on deck as possible. Hold the presses! There is another producer in this mix. Her name is Von Ann Stutler—the wife of the aforementioned Bill.

The Stutlers met in college—she was a singer for a long time, throughout her schooling, then a voice major at Michigan State. Bill was a drum major—a twirler, no less! They met during her freshman year—he had already been there a year. He was a year ahead—but the same age. The marching band always practiced under my dorm. And so the twirlers were around a lot. Frequently after class, I'd go to watch the band. Everybody loved it! I kept seeing this guy, this twirler. In those days, girls could not be in the marching band. It was a 125-all-male band. She was in the concert band. Twirlers led the concert band; so she met this guy. That was the fall of her freshman year. She fell that fall. We were together all the way through college. Bill was from West Virginia; she was from Michigan. She was an hour away from her home; he was eight hours away.

The years went by and they got married after college. We met in 1957; they married in 1962. Bill stayed at the college an extra year (to pick up his BA) until she graduated. Bill couldn't find a job at that point, so Von Ann went back home. Bill got his MA in advertising. He needed experience. There was also the draft hanging over him. Luckily, he had a problem foot, so he wasn't drafted. Funny, Bill marched all over the world—but the US Army wouldn't take him because of his foot. Funny.

Continuing—Von Ann got a job as a psychiatric social worker at Ionia State Hospital for the criminally insane, in a town near Lansing, Michigan. She was the first woman social worker there. She was in a ward with women. She loved that job. That was her college degree. I know—this is just the perfect background to learn how to buy, develop, and run a dinner theatre!

She left her job because Bill was beating the pavement looking for a job. The Stutlers bought a car—she drove it—he went to Chicago and was hired by Miles Laboratories. They were responsible for Alka Seltzer, One A Day vitamins, etc. Bill became an account executive.

When he got the job in January, they picked March 17 to get married. Happy St. Patrick's Day! Von Ann moved to Chicago—no honeymoon—no job for her. She was then hired by the Chicago State Hospital, a very famous place (book written about it!). She now worked with children.

Four years passed. Von Ann got pregnant. Miles Laboratories moved to New York City. So did the three Stutlers. Bill was asked to go with the account. How fantastic! The Stutlers wanted to go to New York anyway! Von Ann's memories were of being raised on a farm. During the bad, lean times, it was farming. She loved it! Unfortunately, as we well know, there is no place in Westchester to have a pet cow, pet horse, or pet pig. Thirty-two people lived in the town with Von Ann's family. Thirty-two.

All through her high school years, her mom talked up New York. (She was born in New Jersey.)

In 1966, the Stutlers moved to Ossining, New York, where a newborn son joined his sister, Von Ann, the mother, and Bill, the father. They moved into their first house, where they had their third child. Now would be a perfect time to build a dinner theatre, dontcha think?

Von Ann's minor in music would now serve her well. As would her background in social work.

At that time, Broadway tickets were $14 each. A bit different than today.

Three producers; three friends: Bill and Von Ann kept talking about it, putting together investors. Nobody at the outset seemed interested. They had their old Victorian house ($27,500 when it was bought.) Bill and Von Ann, Bob—well, you see, they had no money. But they began to put together small investors. You remember the TV show *Mad Men*? On television, with Jon Hamm—that particular episode when Robert Morse, deceased, did a dance . . . Well, at the time both Bob and Bill were accountants—that was the world in New York. Schmoozing dinners . . . drinking . . . schmoozing clients . . . this wasn't the life for the producers. No.

Bob Funking was a city boy. He wasn't a happy accountant. He used to, as a kid, pay for standing-room-only tickets on Broadway. He had the bug even then. He didn't have a lot of money, either. He learned to cook—he became an excellent cook—as we know. So Bill approached Bob Funking with this idea after Bill had approached all his other friends, who turned him down. "That should be noted! Bill actually talked to many other people first up here in Westchester! I was the only fool who said yes!"

So we now have three producers working out of the Stutler living room. Bob lived with the Stutlers the first year. They worked each night. Each day. All three producers were there at the get-go.

They found this space in Elmsford, New York. They told the corporation that owned the property what they wanted to do— i.e., open a dinner theatre. They people were responsive—but not with money.

As usual in any business venture, it is hard to find investors, especially for a novel property such as this! So they asked friends, and they asked relatives. And . . .

Enter: Judith Chafee. She was a woman in a man's field. I'm telling you this because she was a world-renowned architect in a field dominated in the 1970s by men. And she was resented by men—probably because she was better at the job—there was rampant discrimination against women. Believe it? Sure. Believe it. I bet there is still rampant discrimination against women today. I would bet that a woman only makes seventy cents on each dollar that a man makes. I would bet. Wouldn't you? You think?

Now: Judith Chafee, heavily pedigreed:

Her resume, summarized:

Bennington College, Vermont, graduate: BA Visual Arts;
*   Graduate work in Art History and Art Museum*
Yale University School of Architecture
Architects Collaborative, Cambridge
Office of Saarinen and Associates, Hamden
Office of Barnes, New Haven: Project Architect
Independent practice
Member American Institute of Architects
NCARB Certificate

* * *

A party: The men met her. She had just finished designing a house for a wealthy woman, over $100,000—eccentric lady. As Chafee told Bob about this *expensive* house, she said: "You have to realize, this is where she keeps her shoes." She took Bob Funking on a tour of that house. Judith Chafee had a resume you would die for. She got no credit for it—she worked for a large organization, but never got the credit. She had studied with Paul Rudolf and even Walter Gropius in Germany—all huge talents in architecture. She went on her own. She was of the Rhode Island Chafees—so her resume was impeccable. And her talent was, too. Bob asked her if she could design a house for him for $20,000, and she said that she could try. Bob had a piece of property in a field of pine trees. He told her that he "wanted to be up in the trees," so it went straight up!

The builders were skeptical because Judith was a woman— imagine that! One builder redesigned it—where Bill lives now—and it cost $30,000—in early 1970s terms. Why am I telling you this? Read on.

Bob invited Bill and Von Ann to visit his new house, designed by the aforesaid Judith Chafee. "We were like teen-agers!" When they got involved with forming what was to be An Evening Dinner Theatre—they called on Judith Chafee to design it.

Judy and Bob and Bill saw many different dinner theatres—there were so many of them at that time because it was a growing industry—a lot of them were just banquet halls or restaurants. "They just wanted to make some money!" A lot of those places were just set up to stuff people in. She came up with the design. It was so different from the others. And so many, many others are gone . . . finished . . . disappeared . . .

"Money makes the world go around, the world go around, the world go around." *Cabaret***: Fred Ebb and John Kander**

Now what the producers needed was capital—money—dinero—argent. So the next step would be to raise it.

"We can do it! We can do it! We can make a million bucks!" *The Producers:* **Mel Brooks and Thomas Meehan**

Henry Jacobson, who was Oscar Hammerstein's stepson, became interested because Bill and Bob presented their ideas to him. Eventually Dorothy Rodgers became interested. Imagine! They presented their ideas all over the place—even to Sardi's—who stole their ideas to open up their own dinner theatre! I know, I know, you're asking, where is Sardi's dinner theatre today?

Nowhere. They lasted only a year and a half. Serves them right!

But . . . An Evening Dinner Theatre would be born. It would rise!

They made time to put their presentations to the investors who would help them create this dream. Blood, sweat, and tears—as Winston Churchill said. They found thirteen people, who invested $7,500 each, for stock in this new corporation.

The same friend, Ray Ferguson, who had introduced the producers to Judith Chafee, also introduced them to Fred Debetsky, the Port-O-San man! I won't go to the toilet for a joke! No, I won't go to the "potty!" Debetsky's company provided portable potties for many, many places—including Woodstock, so, as you can guess, he was loaded! The idea didn't "flush down the drain."

Debetsky and his three partners, Hymie and Hermie Mindich (brothers) and Lenny Okyle each gave $25,000—their shrewd lawyer said that all of the investors would invest a *loan*—so, yes—all the money would have to be paid back!

Funking and Stutler gambled on their dream. Some of the money went for a loan; some went for the stock in this new company. But, guess what? All that money was paid back with interest in a few years! What business that you know of can brag about that?

These people—their families—still own that stock. All these people liked Funking and Stutler's presentation, so they were interested financially. Money in the early 1970s was insecure. I don't mean that money is insecure—it was just bad times. Bad financial times. Best time to open a dinner theatre. In Elmsford, New York—Westchester. Yup. The Stutlers and Bob Funking had a dream. And their dream propelled them forward and beyond.

"To dream the impossible dream . . . to fight the unbeatable foe . . . to hear with unbearable sorrow . . . to run where the brave dare not go." *Man of La Mancha*: **Joe Darian and Mitch Leigh**

SCENE TWO: "WERE THINE THAT SPECIAL SPACE"

The lights change as we begin our scene. Bill Stutler met accountant Tom Marchetti at a party. This was a monumental occurrence in the life of this new dinner theatre that was to rise in Elmsford, New York. He became their treasurer—with connections for a Small Business Administration loan. They needed $500,000! The SBA came in for $400,000; they raised the rest through small investors. And, as I said, they paid it all back! When there were profits in the old days, the money was distributed, and everybody was happy. So, with this new theatre situation, everybody eventually would be happy. Even Stutler and Funking would be happy. Marchetti said, "We were best friends. I worked with them twelve years. When they needed the money, I got it. They are the best in the theatre business. Through thick and through thin, I would be with them." Marchetti met them through a mutual friend. He had an accounting practice at the time. They had a rough financial plan. From there, they all worked out a business plan.

> **"In ev'ry job that must be done, there is an element of fun; you find the fun and snap! The job's a gem; and ev'ry task you undertake becomes a piece of cake, a lark! A spree! It's very clear to see that . . . A spoonful of sugar helps the medicine go down! The medicine go down, the medicine go down!** *Mary Poppins*: **Richard and Robert Sherman**

Marchetti knew all the ins and outs of the SBA—but it still took a long time for the money to come through. Funking, meanwhile, was on assignment with his ad agency for housewives' presentations—no cell phones, obviously—when the word finally came in! Hallelujah! Both men could now quit their high-paying jobs and invest time, money, and effort in an enterprise that would bring them much lower capital and much bigger headaches. Go figure.

Funking had help with this idea, with an ad agency helper— a woman, a blond, who married a poet. Really. Names? We don't remember. Just a funny thing, really!

The aforesaid Robert Martin Corporation entered the picture. Martin Berger and Robert Weinberg owned this real estate development corporation. They owned the Elmsford property, property in Connecticut, Yonkers, etc. It was a big deal with big dealers.

Meanwhile—back at the ranch—Bob Funking bought the first house in Kemyeys Cove, in Scarborough, New York—built by these guys. Upstairs lived the Schubert family. Talk about hobnobbing it with the rich! And connected! That was the Stutler clan and Bub Funking. Then.

All right. They were all set to build. Stutler and Funking had the backup money, the idea, the place. So? Let's build!

Not yet, folks, not yet. There was the zoning board. There was a hearing. The town supervisor, Tony Veteran, newly elected, to straighten up the place. "Don't let these real estate brokers take over the place!" All of a sudden, there are a lot of objections! Stutler and Funking are putting in a strip joint! Imagine that! How horrible! How terrible! How pointless for the community! How full of bullshit were these objections!

"Let me entertain you, let me make you smile. Let me do a few tricks, some old and then some new tricks, I'm very versatile." *Gypsy*: **Stephen Sondheim and Jule Styne**

They were supposed to open in January 1974—as they tell it: "How stupid we were! Opening a new business in January! There were many hearings. There was one person who spoke up every time against us. As it was said, the guy had such a ballsy job—a bond lawyer—in Manhattan. A very dull job. He always spoke up at the planning board—the zoning board." Billy Hammerstein came in to speak for them. He was the son of Oscar Hammerstein. They had presented to him via his stepbrother, Henry Jacobson (as I mentioned previously), who worked with the producers at Kelly Nason, which was the advertising agency they both worked for. He was a marketing guy and respected by those in the theatrical community. And he was on board with the producers' proposal for a dinner theatre in Elmsford, New York. But wait! This big-mouthed guy at the hearings had the audacity to say, "Oh, now we get all the apple pie coming in!" He, of course, was talking about the scion of the Hammerstein clan.

All of a sudden, Stutler and Funking were the bad Boy Scouts. They were building a brothel! They were upsetting the "countryside!" They were nasty! They were ba-a-a-ad boys! They were told this guy always opposed everything, and Tony Veteran (the head of the board) wasn't for it, either, because he wanted to "clean up the park"—whatever that means. Who can tell about politicians?

Robert Weinberg—their lawyer—did all the negotiations for this. There were many, many, many meetings from January to July, when they finally opened. Finally, it happened! To work. Construction—Judith Chafee designed, and construction by Robert Martin Associates. Imagine! One and one half months till approval finally came through. Rumors still flew! Some people probably thought that Stutler and Funking were building a burlesque theatre—circa 1910. Imagine.

The workmen, being male chauvinists, although they were getting paid, didn't trust Chafee. Remember—she was a woman. Terrible! For them, of course. Not for us, reflecting upon our year of 2021, where women have equal rights and equal pay in jobs. Right.

Most dinner theatres of the time were banquet halls, or in the round, or thrust stage, with a small stage, with lunch tables set up for patrons. Horrible! Nope: An Evening Dinner Theatre would have it different. A miniature UN!—because of the way it was set up. Yup.

The key things Chafee contributed to was the design: a thrust stage; all seats could view the proceedings—and a homey feeling of a wonderful theatre that encompassed you—all around you—for, wherever you sat, you could see the action, the actors, and hear the singing! And have the lighting like that of a Broadway theatre. The original idea was to utilize the space you had. She had to get everything in: 400 seats. An Evening Dinner Theatre, as designed by a *woman*, was unique from many other theatres of the time such as a special seating arrangement—you always faced the stage—there were no 'bad' seats; the stage itself had a three-quarter thrust. At that time (different obviously from 2017), women weren't equal.

These producers decided that the casting of Broadway performers was most important (Equity) at auditions and hiring the creative staff (directors, choreographers, musical directors, set, costume, and lighting designers) in New York City. Imagine!

The Stutlers and Funking contributed time, effort, drive—the main ingredients to An Evening Dinner Theatre—the main thing: DRIVE. This theatre would be the country's only year-round Equity theatre. As one noted producer once said, "We've found that musical comedies are the most popular productions . . . and we have the best subscription deal in the New York area . . . it's the biggest bargain in dining-entertainment around." Anywhere.

You would think that these *producers* could do it by themselves. Oh, no. They had help. They needed help to make sure that The Evening Dinner Theatre would be born. The Stutlers also became guardians of two other children. At this time.

As Von Ann says, in an article by Debbie Wasserman, "Dinner theatre combines the two things we love most. people and performing."

"We raised the money, we're on our way . . . we have our backing. Oh, what a day... . . Wonder of wonders, we have all our cash, barring all blunders, we should have a smash!" *The Producers*

The Stutlers and Mr. Funking had no money of their own. As said. But they had backers. Thank you, Tom Marchetti.

Finally the proposal went through the planning board, finally through the town board, they were bored with the waiting from the boards . . . and, oh—traffic studies . . . "Ooh! There's gonna be so much traffic—they'll be killing people!" There hasn't been one damn accident or one damn death because of traffic. 1974–2017.

Because of that big delay in getting approval, the necessary permits, etc., they ran out of money because of the time it took! Oy! More money had to be raised! Thank you, Tom Marchetti!

Onto another problem: they needed a chef. To the Culinary Institute! There was a list of people looking for jobs. They sent us several people. They hired someone! His name was Joe Staron. He was being paid since January and was responsible for putting together the kitchen. Can you imagine! Everybody, before An Evening Dinner Theatre was finally completed, worked out of Bill Stutler's house—an old Victorian. Their office was in the center of a giant room of the house!

In other dinner theatres, the waiters were also the entertainers. They sang on stage, they acted. And they served. There was a preshow and a show. Stutler and Funking wanted to be union, wanted to be Equity. No waiters singing—too cheesy. They obviously didn't know much about producing, or kitchens, or staff, so they figured it would be a good idea to try to raise money and open a theatre with dinner. Imagine!

They found many people to help them. There was Jack Batman. (More on him later.) He was the first guy who did any casting. Michael Hotopp became the designer of sets and costumes of the original organization that produced their shows (DAHD Productions). Ken Kressel, owner of DAHD Productions—the original producers of the first Evening Dinner Theatre shows— was given a special financial arrangement, arranged by the producers with his company. Ken started casting friends—Bob and Bill said no-no. He was given stock in the company, and when he left, it was returned. Listen, nobody's perfect. The producers realized that they could do it themselves. Hotopp did, however, continue working for them. And so it goes. A family was born. Welcome to An Evening Dinner Theatre. The beginning of the dream of two determined men, conceived by the strength of a dream—in Elmsford, New York.

"The cast is great. The script is swell. But this we're tellin' you, sirs, it's just no go, you got no show, without the Producers!" *The Producers*

SCENE THREE:
HAPPILY EVER AFTER-ING

"A law was made a distant moon ago here. July and August cannot be too hot. And there's a legal limit to the snow here. In Camelot." *Camelot*: **Alan Jan Lerner and Frederick Loewe**

This Camelot became An Evening Dinner Theatre by three producers: Bob Funking and Bill Stutler . . . with Von Ann Stutler as business manager. Because this thought came to Bill, that he liked the combination of theatre and dinner. It has a very relaxed atmosphere, and he liked the idea of not having to go to New York City for a play. You would believe that with such a dream the work would be easy and the theatre would be ready to open on time. Not so! Von Ann told a reporter, "We were still laying carpet the day we opened; we laid the last piece at five o'clock and opened the doors at six fifteen."

The up-and-coming producers wanted the use of imagination—which had been lost through television. It seems, for them—and for us—that theatre makes you use it; you are drawn into it—made to feel a part of the show—that's the magic of theatre. It's true that innovation and creative thinking are necessary for the adaption of audiences to a small theatre. And so it goes, July in the year 1974. The first person they hired was Bruce Lifrieie. He was just out of college, interested in theatre—and young. And bright. Off to Westchester Community College and Mark Clark, the professor. The two producers spoke to all the students in his drama classes. Pia Haas was one of them. (More on her later.)

Now, to put on a show. They had a place. They had personnel. The producers had verve. The producers had drive. The producers had capital, had backers. The producers had permits. The producers had many ideas. The producers had . . . the producers had . . .

The Stutlers had children—eventually all worked in the theatre. Bill's fraternity brother and closest friend, Bill McIntosh, and his wife, Nancy, were close to both Stutlers in college. McIntosh was the advertising account executive on Coke's Tab product. While he was visiting the Stutlers in New York, his wife, Nancy, suddenly died of a brain aneurism. Bill eventually came to live with the Stutlers for a short time before he could find a place on his own. He had two daughters. Unexpectedly, Bill McIntosh died of Hensen's Disease (Leprosy). The Stutlers became foster parents to both of the McIntosh daughters. So, to get this straight, Bill Stutler—with his partner, Bob Funking—was starting out on a business venture. They were beginning An Evening Dinner Theatre. Both producers quit their high-paying jobs to invest in this idea—this dream—this miracle. And Bill and Von Ann Stutler had five mouths to feed, plus their own.

So Von Ann hired this special woman—a mother—to help. And Von Ann was always there at breakfast—and both parents never missed their children's games or other activities, lacrosse, debates, etc. They split it up. They just had to do it—they had plenty of energy. One or the other parent ate dinner with the kids each night. The kids fared well. They had love. They had music. And the kids had their parents' theatre.

In an interview article by Debbi Wasserman, Von Ann is quoted as telling of An Evening Dinner Theatre as a "people-oriented business; more than a restaurant and more than a theatre, you're involved with your customers for an entire evening. You're more involved with them socially. I love that and I love being part of the community. I'm getting to know the people in Westchester and Westchester is where I live."

The article continues. (It was written in 1981.) It tells that about seven years earlier, Von Ann and Bill took stock of their lives: children they loved; a house in Westchester, and the aforementioned *Mad Men* job that Bill had in New York City. It was very necessary to talk about something that they could all do together, where all would not be tied down from nine to five. Happiness would definitely follow. Welcome to An Evening Dinner Theatre.

With Bob Funking aboard, the idea was born. So Von Ann, Bill, and Bob now devoted their professional lives to theatre—in Elmsford, New York. You can imagine that this venture would be a shock to anyone's nervous system.

We now know—and they knew then—that dinner theatre would combine the two things that are loved: people and performing.

So . . . opening night!

"Another op'nin', another show . . . to Philly, Boston or Baltimoe . . . A chance for stage folks to say hello . . . another op'nin' of another show!" *Kiss Me, Kate*: **Cole Porter**

Why do you think they chose *Kiss Me, Kate* as their opening show at An Evening Dinner Theatre? Listen to the song "Another Op'nin', Another Show," from that show, and the song is so representative of a perfect opening night in July of 1974.

Perfect opening, right? Well, according to Leslie Davis: original hostess (you would have loved the gowns), who graduated, first as an original group sales representative, then matinee manager, then executive secretary, then marketing director, and finally, presently retired, the opening wasn't exactly perfect. Before I tell you the *real* story of opening night, just check out the pattern with Ms. Davis. She rose in the An Evening Dinner Theatre family/Westchester Broadway Theatre family to many different positions. That is so true for so many people who were part of that family.

"Some of these jobs I performed at the same time. Group sales bookings in the daytime and hostessing in the evening. Actually, I was a hostess at every performance for the first three years."

More on the Evening Dinner Theatre/Westchester Broadway Theatre family later . . . remember to ask me about the marriages of people who met here, and the Broadway luminaries who graduated from here. You see, the story of An Evening Dinner Theatre/Westchester Broadway Theatre is more than a business. Yes, it's more than a wonderful place for musical theatre in Westchester. Yes, it's more. It's a place for family—many families—many loyalties, many years. Many years. But now, back to opening night, according to Ms. Davis:

"July 9, 1974, a hot air balloon was to hover over the theater with spotlights on the huge An Evening Dinner Theatre logo. However, winds aloft did not permit this happening, and the balloon sat in a nearby parking lot that night."

Wonder what that cost?

The balloon was aloft a few days later!

"The carpeting in the lobby was being nailed in place right up to the doors of the lobby just moments before the first guests arrived. The whole evening ran extraordinarily well; however, we neglected to collect any admissions from the paying customers in our focus to have everything work smoothly!" You might enter the producers' minds at the time and think: "Well, we may not make a go of it, but we'll have had one hell of a party!"

The party began that night. That's why they called it "An Evening Dinner Theatre!"

Let's turn to Ray Ferguson. He knew Bob previously, so when they were raising funds, he became an original investor. He gave money to the project. He also found more investors, which probably put them over the top! Nice guy! They were friends.

Von Ann in October of 1973, at the beginning of their fundraising. Friends. "Von Ann was very active in the formation of this theatre . . . Bill and Bob were partners."

Bob was his friend—and then he became a friend of Bill's! He realized that they were going to cater to an audience that liked dinner and theatre. That was the risk; but they succeeded! He did their marketing and advertising in 1981. He was president of an advertising agency, and "they returned the loyalty to me." You see, loyalty—a big part of this story.

Remember Tom Marchetti: "I had an accounting practice in Poughkeepsie at the time. A friend referred Bob and Bill to me for dinner theatre funding. I secured a CPA loan. Howard Fein, a lawyer, and Sol Bromberg negotiated an SBA line of credit to get the whole dinner theatre thing started. I negotiated Equity positions for other investors and secured a lease with Robert Martin Company and got the Actors Equity contract.

"Then I assisted in outfitting and staffing the facility. I worked with Joe Staron, executive chef, to purchase kitchen equipment. Then I was asked to take a more active role in operations as treasurer and board member.

"I worked with Bill and Bob on a two-day rotation, seven days a week, running this theatre. We did this for five or six years until it was profitable."

What about food? Uh-oh! They didn't get permission to open their restaurant on time from the powers that be! What to do?

Enter Ed Hawkins, owner of Reiber's Restaurant in Elmsford.

"A very strange way to help . . . Bill and Bob used to eat in my restaurant while they were waiting for approval of the municipality. They were turned down. They came into the restaurant forlorn. "What do you mean, you were turned down?" Hawkins called up the head of the board. "What ya do this for? It's the greatest use of commercial space around."

They had another meeting and he spoke at that meeting in their behalf. Tony Veteran, town supervisor, asked him why he was there at that meeting. "I am for the project!"

Hawkins spoke on their behalf. And he spoke thus: "You can vote now on the approval, or I will give you a six-hour dissertation on it." Ha! What do you think happened? Then he invited everybody back to Reiber's for a drink. Problem solved. It helps to have friends.

Now, the opening: Bill and Bob came to Ed Hawkins and said they had to cancel because the board of health hadn't approved their kitchen yet. And Ed said, "I can cater it! I can do all the cooking here!" For a couple of nights he sent food over!

"Another op'nin,' another show!" *Kiss Me, Kate*: Cole Porter

Ed said of Bill and Von Ann and Bob: "That was a long time . . . they were good people." They still are, and Ed Hawkins is eighty-two years old. He doesn't sound like eighty-two years old. His memory, like Bob and Bill's, are exact. "A good memory."

Well, as Bob Funking has said, "After forty-two years, I'm still here!" Yes, right there in Elmsford—at An Evening Dinner Theatre.

How to get to opening night: the advertising agency—Kelly Naison—where the producers had worked previously, were very supportive (Jerry Shoenfeld of Tarrytown, especially) volunteered to do advertising! Indeed, on opening night, the people from the agency sent a busload of people to see it!

The large, full-page ad in the *Westchester Journal News* states:

* * *

"NOW BROADWAY COMES TO WESTCHESTER with the first professional dinner-theatre in Westchester! You're invited to *Kiss Me, Kate!* Sit in relaxed comfort in swivel chairs—7 levels make every seat closer than 45 feet to the stage. Enjoy Cole Porter's *Kiss Me, Kate*, running for six weeks. "An Evening": Superb dinner at 6:30, exciting theater at 8:30. All year round, all under one roof, all for one price. Only $10.95 weekdays, $12.95 Friday, Saturday, Sunday. Free Parking. Subscription rate and group rates available. Charge cards or personal check accepted. Phone for reservations . . ."

A quote on the ad: "Westchester's newest dinner-theater opened to a full house Tuesday night with a beautifully, professionally staged *Kiss Me, Kate*. Cole Porter's musical comedy of life backstage in a theatrical troupe touring with Shakespeare's *Taming of the Shrew* struck the right notes as an introduction to the elegant contemporary building in the Cross-Westchester Executive Park in Elmsford behind the Ramada Inn."

Starring in this performance in July of 1974 were: Virgil Curry (114 city tour of *Applause*; Gloria Zaglool (Hodel opposite Zero Mostel); Richard Ryder (of *Oh Calcutta*) and Larry Whiteley (directed national tour of *Godspell*.)

"Things look swell, things look great, gonna have the whole world on a plate, starting here, starting now, honey, ev'ry thing's coming up roses! *Gypsy*: **Jule Styne**

Alumni from that show included Richard Casper, who was a chorus kid in *Kiss Me, Kate*. He eventually became a very successful director (more on him later). Unfortunately, he succumbed to AIDS. The lobby at Westchester Broadway Theatre is dedicated to him.

Gloria Zaglool eventually went into some religious cult: "We never saw the lead every again."

The show did 69 percent capacity—they only did it for six weeks. They did realize that as a new business it would take time for audiences to build. Each producer took a salary; they split the nights; one each was there for the eight shows—they didn't have matinees in the beginning.

A little old lady convinced the producers to add a matinee; she had run Casino Royale. Now she ran group sales. What a business! Irma Cronin was her name. She had developed a following in that catering place of senior citizens, and now was a welcome addition to An Evening. After we opened, that place opened the Tuckahoe Dinner Theater. It failed. But a matinee audience didn't! Irma brought in busloads of senior citizens for matinees! Her lists of seniors brought them business! An Evening became A Matinee!

Today *Hamilton* takes in 3.3 million dollars a show ($250 a ticket). Imagine! It's 1974, the price for dinner, parking, and show was miniscule (as it is today,) compared to Broadway. Imagine!

And you know, in order to put on a show, you must first purchase the rights from an organization. In 1974, almost immediately after a show closed on Broadway, the Stutlers and Mr. Funking could get the rights immediately. Today, in 2016, it's impossible to get rights to such shows as *Jersey Boys* because touring companies have the rights locked up. Forget *Les Miserables*—Cameron McIntosh is planning to bring it back to Broadway every three years!

But—wait a minute—that's today. We're back in 1974, remember?

The producers alternated a comedy with each musical. But the comedies didn't sell at all. Nope. So, An Evening Dinner Theatre became a Musical Evening Dinner Theatre.

Did people in the area embrace An Evening when it opened? Well? Did they draw from Westchester? It depends.

Barefoot in the Park only lasted five mediocre weeks.

I know you're asking, how did Von Ann, Bill Stutler (and family), and Bob Funking live? On what salary? Well, the theatre paid them the enormous sum of $25,000 a year. Anyone could live on that, right? Wait—it's 1974.

The cost for admission was $11.82. Then it went to $13.61. It never got above $14.00. That was a *fortune* for an evening or a matinee at An Evening Dinner Theatre!

Giancarlo Esposito is an actor. But first he was a busboy. More stories, more anecdotes. If you run such a family business as An Evening Dinner Theatre, you get stories. Many stories. "There isn't a show on Broadway today that doesn't have at least one alumna from our theatre." And that probably is true!

But back to Giancarlo Esposito. His brother was a waiter; he was a concert violinist. He was also a singer. But he was a busboy. His mother was an opera singer of no great renown. She once sang the national anthem! Off-key!

And now an article from the *New York Post* of Saturday, February 11, 2017, about the same Mr. Giancarlo Esposito, who once was a busboy in Elmsford, New York:

BREAKING GOOD
Confidential *with Brian Niemietz*

Giancarlo Esposito, who played terrifying *Breaking Bad* drug lord Gus Fring, shows his soft side in a video promoting the city's "One Book, One New York" campaign, encouraging New Yorkers to vote on a book that the entire city will read at the same time. "I would be very disappointed if my book didn't win," Esposito says, while cuddling a teddy bear in the ad. His pick: *The Sellout* by Paul Beatty. The initiative was announced by Commissioner of Media and Entertainment Julie Menin; voting runs until Feb. 28.

After the shows in the early days of An Evening, there would be an aftershow for the cast and interested investors and friends. They never went home! Imagine! A piano cabaret! Giancarlo got up one day and sang. He had an incredible voice! He graduated to An Evening's *South Pacific.*

Just to give you an idea of the influence of the Stutler's and Funking's An Evening Dinner Theatre, take one individual by the name of Giancarlo Esposito, a busboy in the mid-1970s at An Evening Dinner Theatre.

His biography is amazing: He was born in Copenhagen, Denmark, to an Italian carpenter/stagehand father from Naples and an opera-singing African American mother from Alabama. His parents moved to Manhattan by the time he was six, and that's where he grew up. At the age of eight, he had already appeared on Broadway as a slave child in *Maggie Flynn.* The year was 1966. Then he was a busboy at An Evening Dinner Theatre; then a "star" on their thrust stage.

Eventually he went to Broadway and movies and television. From the television series *Homicide: Life on the Street* he won two Obie Awards, and he was a member of the jury at the Sundance Film Festival. Then he went to *Breaking Bad* and received a star on the Hollywood Walk of Fame in 2014.

Such a wonderful career, and it began on the stage in Elmsford—at An Evening Dinner Theatre.

One night, after a show, a lady called and said that her husband was missing his glass eye. It had been bothering him, so he put it on the parapet and left it there. At the end of the show, the waiters were cleaning up. The producers asked the waiters to look for it. They looked and couldn't find it. Then . . . Bob told the woman that "We will continue looking for it—we'll keep an *eye* out for it." Ha!

The next day the cleaning person let out a scream. She kept an eye out and found the eye between the bottom of the parapet wall and the carpet. She *eyed* it!

"Eye've Got the Sun in the Morning and the Moon at Night: *Annie Get Your Gun*: **Irving Berlin**

SCENE FOUR:
LUCK BE A LADY, TONIGHT!

From "The Gourmet Game" by Elliott Loebl, *Show Business Newspaper*, July 21, 1974: "An international buffet table, featuring over 60 hot and cold items, and one of my favorite Broadway shows, "Kiss Me Kate" presented in comfortable theatre atmosphere, made an enjoyable weekend for this reporter.

"An Evening is the name of this professional dinner-theatre located in Westchester county at the Cross Westchester Executive Park, in Elmsford.

"The owners, Robert Funking, and William Stutler, after two years of working on the project, have opened a dinner theatre facility that is the best I have ever attended. The unique interior has been designed on seven levels, which provides for a clear view of the thrust stage and allows all customers to eat and watch the show from the same table . . .

"Open daily, except Monday, for dinner and theatre. Cost is $10.95 plus tax on Tuesday-Thursdays, and $12.95 plus tax on Friday-Sunday. Specialties include the Roast Beef, Seafood combinations, and Chicken."

Ah, it is indeed, a theatre—a dinner theatre at that. If I were an angel hovering over Elmsford, New York, I'd recall that the following people owe allegiance, in some way, to Bob Funking, Von Ann and Bill Stutler.

Ah, the memories . . . of Iris Revson, George Puleo, Tom Ulrich, Mark McGrath, Glory Crampton (eighteen at her start at An Evening), Carol Woods, Liz Larsen, Richard Matby, Jr., Jason Graae, Vicki Lewis, Walter Bobbie, Randy Graff, Kurt Peterson, Paige O'Hara, Estelle Harris, Ron Holgate, Jack Batman, Charles Repole, Susan Stroman, John Lloyd Young, Kathleen Marshall, Rob Marshall, Rob Ashford, Tommie Walsh,

Randy Skinner, Scott Bakula, Joan Rivers, Woody Herman, Tommy Dorsey's Band, The Shirelles, The Clancy Brothers, Don Imus, The Amazing Kreskin, Mickey Gilley, Robert Cuccioli, (or course) Giancarlo Esposito, Stan Kenton, Ilene Graff, Maury Yeston—and many more celebrities (musicians, actors, directors, Broadway and Hollywood icons)—all got their start because of Bob Funking, Von Ann and Bill Stutler. These are some of An Evening Dinner Theatre/Westchester Broadway Theatre's alumni family. And there are more! Yes . . . read on, ladies and gentlemen, read on! Imagine! I dare anyone, across this grand country, to duplicate the influence of this theatre—any morning, any afternoon, any *evening*!

Do you remember *Annie* on Broadway? Well, the part of Arvide Abernathy was played, at An Evening Dinner Theatre, by Reid Shelton—the original Daddy Warbucks. Really.

An Evening Dinner Theatre's menu was more diverse: a gourmet buffet. Different kinds of exotic dishes were served. Eventually, Stutler and Funking went to a normal buffet. They had what's called a Steamship Round, with a carver who carved different meats. Now you think that chef/restaurant manager was an easy job. Not really. There was Tony Simmons—chef for twenty-five to thirty years. Eventually they had to "get rid of him." By firing, of course—not any crass assassination! You see, he was screwing around with the waitresses. Can't have that!

Next chef was the biggest drug dealer in the county. He was a full-time worker, gambler, constantly in money problems . . . borrowing from employees. He got loads of money from drugs—he even had his children working for him! One day, in a fit of anger, Bob Funking actually backed him up against the wall! Really! And you thought that a dinner theatre was all fun and games! Ha!

This drug dealer made a deal with the DA and ratted on people to save himself. They let him out. Then he went back into dealing drugs. Back to prison. It must be in the genes: his daughter was on the Yonkers City Council and was convicted of fraud. What a family!

Tony Dinis, their new carver, moonlighted with them. "Bill, I can do this job! I can keep my other job as well." Finally at WBT, he came to work full-time—and then came the change to full dinners. You know why? Probably because: "Men hate buffets." You know who came? Groups of firemen came with wives, police . . . they hated it . . . they hated it . . . carpenters, laborers, they didn't want to stand in line, they wanted to be served. So, the producers tested a full dinner vs. the buffet idea. So today they serve full dinners! Stories from the Theatre Zone!

Look around. How many dinner theatres are around today? Sometimes life can get you down, even from producers. Bill could've thought that he has done nothing with his life. But you can imagine Bob answering, "What the hell you talking about—something the community loves and needs—an accomplishment, even if we haven't made a lot of money!" Stories from the Theatre Zone!

Back to the buffet: Would you believe this? A doctor. License plates. A doctor. The family brought shopping bags to the buffet. The father had his preteen children stuff these bags, collecting food, putting it in containers. They stole beef, beef, and beef. What's the beef, you ask? I dunno.

During the meal, this doctor instructed his boys to go back with fresh plates, getting beef. Someone caught on: "Keep your eyes on those people." Plates empty! Beef wrapped! The kids went to the car with loads of beef during intermission! But during the second act, Bill had waiters pry open the door of the doctor's car and take the beef back! They watched as the doctor/father opened the trunk at the end of the show. No more beef! The doctor slapped his kids! And you thought it was easy running a dinner theatre in Westchester!

"Food, glorious food! We're anxious to try it. Three banquets a day. Our favorite diet. Just picture a great big steak, fried, roasted, or stewed! Oh food! wonderful food! marvelous food! glorious food! *Oliver*: Lionel Bart

"An Evening to Remember" was an article in the *Park Life Magazine* (A Robert Martin Magazine) from June 1983, talks of the past nine years: "What began almost ten years ago as a dream of a former dancer and singer, and her ad-executive husband, has been turned into "An Evening" to remember.

"According to Von Ann Stutler, vice president of sales for An Evening Dinner Theatre at 11 Clearbrook Road in the Cross Westchester Executive Park, the idea of opening a dinner-theater in Westchester came about while she was visiting friends in the south. They took her out one night to a local dinner theatre and she was very impressed.

"Joining Ms. Stutler and her husband Bill, who is the theater's producer, was Bob Funking, who became the theater's business manager."

The article continued. "Our use of imagination has been lost through television," said Stutler. "Theater makes you use it, you are drawn into it, made to feel a part of the show—that's the magic of theater. Innovative, creative thinking goes into adaption to the small theater," explained Stutler, who has seen a one-time dream become a reality in An Evening, in Elmsford, N.Y."

In 1974, the producers thought they would alternate comedies with their musicals, so they ran, after *Kiss Me Kate, Barefoot in the Park, Guys and Dolls, The Fantastiks, Blithe Spirit,* and *Play it Again, Sam.* The musicals drew in big crowds to An Evening Dinner Theatre; the comedies did not. So, henceforth, an Evening Dinner Theatre would be presenting only musicals: too many to list here, but from 1974 to February 1991, they produced eighty-three shows. If you divide the years An Evening existed, they put on an average of five full productions each year! Imagine! From *I Do, I Do,* in 1974, to *Me and My Girl,* in 1991. There were: *Man of La Mancha, Oklahoma! Pajama Game, Bells Are Ringing, South Pacific, Anything Goes, Damn Yankees, Annie Get Your gun, Carousel, Can-Can, The Sound of Music, George M! Camelot, Gypsy, Showboat, Fiddler on the Roof, Shenandoah, Pippin, West Side Story, The Music Man, Funny Girl, Hello Dolly! Chicago, No, No, Nanette, Oli-*

ver! Meet Me in St. Louis, Annie, Cabaret, Joseph, Promises, Promises, Baby, Nine, Evita, The King and I, Sugar Babies, My Fair Lady, Dreamgirls, 42nd Street, Big River. It's like a cornucopia of American musical theatre at the end of the twentieth century! Imagine! All these shows were Equity-sanctioned and fantastically produced with professional actors, sets, music, etc. Imagine!

You know why it was so successful, at An Evening Dinner Theatre? "You have to hire the right director, the right choreographer, musical director—they have to be prepared when they get in here. You have to have the schedule laid out right away. Then they can put the show together correctly. They can still adapt to changes. We've been operating this way for forty years, and it works!"

One year, long ago, they hired a choreographer who wasn't prepared. He wanted to create from the beginning. They fired him the second day.

They made money—these producers. And they provided entertainment for Westchester and environs. As you remember, when they first started out they were new. No matinees. They managed to keep going along. The major investors contributed.

Guys and Dolls took off. And so did this show business.

They added specials. A bass player—from the Count Basie Orchestra—he was with that orchestra for many years—told the producers, "You should put together a show with some of the members of this orchestra!" Then there were Irish shows—they were so combative—the audiences—anti-British.

December 1974, the Glenn Miller Orchestra played on one off-night from the major show. Mickey Gilley . . . Duke Ellington . . . Stan Katz . . . Lionel Hampton . . . The Clancy Brothers . . . it went on and on and on.

Charity from the producers Funking and Stutler began at the very outset. Fifty-fifty raffles from audiences provided money for children's gifts for orphanages (how they were named at that time). They gave a free show to orphans. Presents. They maintained this idea each and every year. From these producers. And there are more. Yes!

In 1976 they had a night of operetta. "Try to sell that now!" Almost all of the 400 seats were sold.

The struggle began in 1974. People weren't coming. The economy went down and affected them each year. The economy was poor in 1991 when they moved to new digs. It seemed to be a pattern with these producers. Find a year when the economy was bad, and then open a theatre.

These producers obviously had to have some kind of help. They hired people who mirrored their drive, their joie de vivre, their love of theatre.

"If you change your mind, I'm the first in line, honey, I'm still free, take a chance on me. If you need me, let me know, gonna be around if you got no place to go . . . honey, I'm still free, take a chance on me." *Mamma Mia:* **Benny Anderson, Bjorn Ulvaeus, and Stig Anderson**

There was Richard Caspar: He joined the first show in the ensemble. He was a dancer and a singer. "We met him, liked him—he knew everybody, we partied with him." He did a number of shows for the Stutlers and Funking; he choreographed, then went into directing, an excellent showman. He became their resident director. He worked very fast—under specific time limits. He was a terrific guy, with a sense of humor; all casts loved him. The reason there is a plaque dedicated to him in the lobby is that he worked so long for An Evening/Westchester Broadway Theatre, it's as if he was sent to the producers to make their theatre a success. Unfortunately, he died of AIDS in 1989. He was a great part of their success. He was dedicated to the producers, and they to him.

Caspar got a show ready fast. Today, they close one show after the Sunday matinee and open a new one at the Thursday matinee. In those days, they closed after the Sunday night show and opened at the Wednesday matinee. Caspar got shows up in a day and a half. He was amazing. He was a dedicated soul.

Take Bob Fitzimmons, who worked in both buildings. He was Mr. Westchester. He was a director of a lot of local theatre; he wrote many shows, especially children's. He was the first PR guy for An Evening. He also managed the box office. He also coauthored the current Christmas show. He was a man of terrific talent—you always wanted to have him around you. He was always positive. Unfortunately, he died of a heart attack at a very young age. He was one of the producers' biggest assets. He did everything—everything you wanted or needed to be done, he did it. He knew everybody in theatre community in the area. Another one taken too soon.

There is George Puleo. George, unfortunately, had a stroke. But he's still here. He directed a lot of shows at An Evening/Westchester Broadway Theatre. He directed and ran the Mahopac Farm Playhouse. The producers did a lot of things to stay open during the years, and George was a part of it. Their specials (mystery, *Deathtrap*, for instance) ran for one or two weeks on a Monday and a Tuesday night. They adapted shows, put scenery in the back from the current show, and ran a new show. George was a great part of that.

There was one year during the last couple of years when they were very successful. *Me and My Girl* ran for twenty-six weeks. That was the last one at An Evening Dinner Theatre. Yes, after eighty-three shows. After creating a great influence in Westchester and its environs. After running fifty-two weeks each and every year. Who could match these producers in the quality and quantity of their theatre's work? No one that I can think of.

"From this moment on, You for me, dear, Only two for tea, dear, From this moment on. From this happy day, No more blue songs, Only whoop-dee-doo songs, From this moment on." *Kiss Me, Kate*: **Cole Porter**

Here are some raves from an article by Seema Weinberg:

Gary D. Chattman

DINNER AND THEATRE UNDER ONE ROOF
DESERVES A ROUND OF APPLAUSE!
By Seema Weinberg.

Much more than meets the eye is going on behind the scenes at Westchester's new dinner theatre. "An Evening," located in the Robert Martin Executive Park complex in Elmsford. The owners, architects, producers and directors, chefs, hostesses, waiters and waitresses have all worked with heart and soul to bring about the success of this yet infant enterprise, and they are constantly rewarded by the verbal and written "Superb comments of the audience."

When "An Evening" opened its doors on July 9, 1974, with the production "Kiss Me, Kate," two bright and ambitious young men, William B. Stutler and Robert J. Funking, launched the first dinner theatre in the 914 area with many innovations not to be found in any of the 150 such setups throughout the country. The theatre which accommodates 400 patrons is designed so that no table is no more than forty feet from the stage. All the tables are built on the cantilever principle and face the stage, thus eliminating the problem of having to peer over someone's head. The three-sided thrust stage affords the audience an eye-opening view of the attractive, professional casts. Sitting through a few hours of dinner and performance is also made easy on other parts of the anatomy with the addition of comfortable, high-back swivel chairs.

Both Westchester residents, Bob and Bill plan to continue bringing musicals and comedies to their dinner theatre.

SCENE FIVE:
LULLABY OF BROADWAY

Partners for life: Bill Stutler, Von Ann Stutler, and Bob Funking. The shows at An Evening Dinner Theatre. Loyal staff. Returning directors. Returning actors. Returning set designers.

For instance: Michael Bottari and Ronald Case. Today, 2017, they are Scenic & Costume Designers & Costume Company. I'll let them tell you: "We started designing for Bill Stutler and Bob Funking way back in 1976, just two seasons after they opened what was then called An Evening Dinner Theatre. We remember thinking, what an intimate stylish place to watch theatre, especially musicals.

"We sat at a side table, so we knew right away how very important it was to design for those side seats. Back then, we built and painted our own sets in a small rehearsal room with the help of the technical director, but we have always built our own costume designs (we now have our own costume company).

"We worked there on and off since 1976, designing a few Broadway shows, national tours, and even a Hollywood movie in between. Some of our most rewarding shows were created with the late director Richard Casper and now with the incredible Richard Stafford. There have been other good directors we worked with there, but these two gentlemen allowed us to do our best work while still keeping their vision.

"Since then (and we were honored to design the very first production at the new Westchester Broadway Theatre), they have a great scene shop that builds and paints the sets to our plans and a great in-house prop designer and crew, so we no longer have to do it all ourselves! One thing about this theatre that is different from the others is that the designers can do what they feel is right without interference, provided it is within the budget. Having designed over thirty musicals over the years, we wish the very best for their future." You can't buy loyalty.

There was the show *Pajama Game*:

It ran at An Evening Dinner Theatre from January of 1976 to February of 1976. The entire production was directed and choreographed by John Montgomery, and it stared David Holliday, Bob Gorman, and Carol Swarbrick. Richard Caspar was also in the cast, as was Andy Hostetller. David Holliday's longest-running role on Broadway was that of Richard Kiley's alternate as Don Quixote in *Man of La Mancha,* playing Don Quixote in matinees and Dr Carrasco in the evening performances, from 1965 to 1971 His next performance, as Georges in *Coco,* (1969–1970) earned him a Theatre World Award. Holliday, in London, played Glad Hand and Tony in *West Side Story.*

Bob Gorman today is a nightclub singer. Carol Swarbrick today is a television actress, known for *Like Father, Like Son* (1987); *Norma Jean & Marilyn* (1996) and *Skinflint: A Country Christmas Carol* (1979). Andy Hostetller is a stage manager and a Broadway performer.

Bottari and Case did the scenery. Jack Batman was the publicist. Now he has just coproduced the new Broadway hit, *Natasha, Pierre and The Great Comet of 1812,* with Josh Groban.

In the second scene, they had very heavy sewing machines. They were real! They all fell! The show had to be stopped.

Kurt Peterson starred in many plays for An Evening Dinner Theatre. Then he went on to *Follies* and *Dear World* on Broadway and eventually *The Dark Knight* in the movies. In 1975, he began as *Tom Jones* on An Evening's stage. Then came *I Do, I Do,* opposite Patricia Bruder, from television's *As the World Turns*. Only quality here in Elmsford!

Take *Fiddler on the Roof.* It was a matinee. A senior citizen thought it would be a good idea to go on stage and pat Tevye (during the very serious song "Anatevka") and ask Tevye where the men's room was. Tevye obliged—pointed for the senior. Without missing a beat. Honest.

During the show *Camelot,* we found the changing areas for the actors were in the buffet area of the cafeteria. Quick

change—customers could come out to go to the bathroom. One customer found himself completely outfitted as Lancelot! Surprise!

Lancelot himself looked for his costume change!

For the original incantation of the present Christmas show, the inn in question had furniture that was covered—just like in *Holiday Inn*. In this incarnation, the woman who owned the inn was a large African American lady. She sat down on the furniture, when *screech!* She sat on the theatre cat! Well! The cat got up, looked at her nastily, and promptly existed stage left. During the intermission, guests marveled at the training of this particular cat—to act that way during the show!

There are many stories in the Broadway city—these are but a few! They had a former Miss America in *Cabaret.* They had a former opera singer in *Showboat.*

You can see that the motto here was to find the right people, that's the only way. To work here and keep it going . . . and that is what they were able to do. They got very good people who developed and learned and got better working here at what they did. Like Caspar . . . like Repole . . . like Puelo. Repole was nominated for a Tony—he worked together with Scott Bakula.

Influence. Sitting back—any Westchesterite interested in theatre might say that there'd be no Broadway today without Bill Stutler and Bob Funking.

Marriages. People met there. People got married. Twenty-five. Whole families have worked here. Brother brought in brother; the Jumpers had five brothers who worked there. One now is a school principal; one now is a heart surgeon. Great training from An Evening Dinner Theatre. More on this later!

People: from Westchester Community College Drama Program. They learned here; they grew in theatre here. An Evening Dinner Theatre begot the careers and futures of many a soul.

They booked from King Broder all special evenings at An Evening. He lived to ninety-four. Great guy! He could book you anything, from a flea circus to Pavarotti on the same bill. He was the live *Broadway Danny Rose.* On his glasses he had a crown. He got *Saturday Night Live* for Eddie Murphy. King was one of the great theatre characters of all time. He was amazing. His son, Mitch Broder, is now running this business.

Here is a letter from Dorothy Hammerstein!

> *Dear Mr. Stutler,*
>
> *I was sorry to leave early last night because "Okla-homa" was so wonderful—but I had all sorts of exercises to do before bed because of my disc. I can't tell you how thrilled I was by the performance of all the cast—and I mean ALL the cast. I had no idea that it would all seem so fresh after so many years. If it was cut, I didn't see where—apart from my happiness at the show, I enjoyed the whole place and the dinner too. Thank you for a wonderful evening.*
>
> *Sincerely,*
> *Dorothy Hammerstein*

Take *Annie Get Your Gun*: Irving Berlin, for instance. It ran August 1976–September 1976.

It starred Ilene Graff, John Almberg, Charles Maggiore, and Howard Mann. John Anania played Colonel Buffalo Bill. Ilene Graff originally replaced Carole Demas as "Sandy" in the original Broadway production of *Grease* for two and a half years. Then she went on to *Mr. Belvedere* in 1985, *Loving Annabelle* in 2006, and *Ladybugs* in 1992.

John Almberg appeared on Broadway in *Seesaw* in 1973 and *Mack and Mabel* in 1974.

Lynn Stuart, before becoming a Broadway producer, was in *Kismet, Bells Are Ringing, High Spirits,* and *Portofino.*

Charles Maggiore appeared on Broadway in *Sly Fox* and *Spofford.*

John Anania appeared on Broadway in seven productions, including *Applause, Golden Rainbow,* and in 1978, the revival of *Hello, Dolly.*

The choreographer Peter J. Humphrey choreographed, on Broadway, *Do I Hear a Waltz, Sugar* (with Bobby Morse), *Cabaret,* and *The Boyfriend.*

Gary D. Chattman

The *Journal News* touted: ANNIE HITS A BULLS-EYE!

Imagine! All these Broadway stars appeared in Elmsford at An Evening Dinner Theatre. And there were more . . .

Carousel: September-November 1976. You know that the idea of any business is to make money, correct? But with the Stutlers and Mr. Funking, not only were they good businessmen, good theatre people, but *good people*. See:

DIABETES PARTY AT THEATRE:
(From *The Journal News*)

"A theatre-dinner party to see the revival of the hit show CAROUSEL is being sponsored by the Westchester Diabetes Association on Friday, October 8th. Funds raised will be used to expand patient and community service programs of the Diabetes Association.

"Tickets to the show, at 'An Evening Dinner Theatre' in Elmsford, are available from the Westchester Diabetes Association (914 948-0035) and are tax deductible. Dinner will be served at 6:45 p.m. and the show will begin at 8:30 p.m.

"The Westchester Association, a chapter of the New York Diabetes Association, serves people with diabetes—the third-largest cause of death by disease—through programs of patient counseling and education, research, support, professional education, public information and detection."

And Stutler and Funking did this sort of thing ALL THE TIME!.Believe it!

***

And Rita Rudner—yes, that Rita Rudner—the famous comedian, was in *Can-Can* at An Evening Dinner Theatre in November 1976–January 1977. We all know that before her comedic career, in addition to being part of *Can-Can*, Ms. Rudner had appeared on Broadway in 1972 in *Promises, Promises,* and also in *The Magic Show, So Long 177th Street,* and she was the replacement for the part of Lily St. Regis in the original *Annie* from 1977-1983. As it is told by the producers, Rita Rudner tried out her comedy act simultaneously to appearing at An Evening Dinner Theatre. We all know where that career ended up!

I find this fascinating . . . a history of An Evening Dinner Theatre/Westchester Broadway Theatre is a journey into the history of American musical theatre. Period.

Here is a list of stars that could fit into an atmospheric constellation: *Fantastiks:* Reid Shelton; *Blithe Spirit:* Holland Taylor*; Play It Again, Sam/Tom Jones*: Kurt Peterson.

Stage: Joan Rivers; The Shirelles, Tony Dorsey, Woody Herman, The Clancy Brothers, Don Imus, Amazing Kreskin.

George Lee Andrews, Kevin Gray, Tom Urich, Davis Gaines, George Dvorsky, Mike Burstyn, Dorothy Stanley, PJ Benjamin, Kevin Ramsey, Roz Ryan, Bobby Daye, Carolee Carmello, Paige O'Hara, Kathleen Marshall, Bobby Longbottom, Randy Skinner; Scott Bakula, Estelle Harris, Vicki Lewis, Alexander Chapman, Alan Sues, Yvette Freeman, Holland Taylor, Betsy Palmer, Dorothy Collins . . . and many others!

Back to the beginning of An Evening Dinner Theatre: it had to start somewhere, like the very first employee, whom I have previously mentioned. His name: Bruce Lifrieri. His story: "I was the very first employee. The producers had seen me when, at a cast party, they approached me. Bob Funking had developed this idea that the producers wanted people who worked on the floor and in theatre. That was me. They approached me to work for them.

"At that time, they were just literally digging a hole for the foundation. The year was 1973. I began as a waiter—a cocktail waiter, for their buffet. I served thirty people coffee and drinks. There was a bus person who worked with each waiter in each section. I quickly became the dining room manager, for they had no one else . . . it happened within that first year. All the staff at that time was very young, twenty-ish.

"The nicest thing about working there was that all my siblings came and worked there with me. It was a family-within-a-family! All my brothers worked there. There were many others—the Taggarts—there were five people in their family, all working at An Evening Dinner Theatre! There were the Jumpers! Five boys. As I said, it was a special place to work—people wanted to work there. I met lifelong friends there. You see, the place was doing very well then, back in the seventies. For a young kid—me—I was also doing very well. It was a sort of heaven. Many marriages came about. We, being young men, always were scoping out girls. There were lots of musicals, every six weeks brought a new slew of dancers. I, with my friends, always became friendly with the people in shows. As I said, it was definitely a fun place to work.

"In 1980 I left to open my own restaurant. Working with Bob and Bill was a great learning experience; it built my knowledge from the ground up. After two years, I left my restaurant. I was too young to be so responsible.

"Now, I'm with the New York Rangers, as a medical trainer. You just don't know what path you will take when you're young. But, without a doubt, the family at An Evening Dinner Theatre put my on the right path."

One might say that to build a family within An Evening Dinner Theatre, it takes a village. Take Leslie Davis, one of the original hostesses (you would have loved the gowns). She was original group sales representative, matinee manager, executive secretary, marketing director. Today she is retired.

I'm sure you could guess that in the beginning to get such a tremendous enterprise as a dinner theatre started, everything was new and hard. Leslie performed some of the jobs at the same time. She did group sales bookings in the daytime and hostessed in the evening. "Actually, I was a hostess at every performance for the first three years."

Let me let her tell you her thoughts: "Personally, I do not think 'miracle' is the correct word for so much hard work. For starters, none of us had ever done this type of work before, and there was a huge learning curve and many tweaks to everything before we knew what the heck we were doing.

"Initially, we did not have matinees. These came about because a 'little old lady' met with Bill and Bob along with her shopping bags filled with contacts to senior citizen groups over a tri-state area and convinced them she could fill every seat at every show.

"Her name was Irma Cronin. She did keep her word on that. Her prior experience was with Murrays Parkway Casino in Tuckahoe, once owned by her brother. And she did fill every matinee." I repeated this just for effect—and to corroborate what I wrote before!

Think for just a moment. You have two account executives: Bob Funking, and Bill Stutler and Von Ann Stutler, Bill's wife. They raised capital to build a dinner theatre. They fought ordinances and red tape, and then built An Evening Dinner Theatre in Elmsford. Then they hired staff for this place. Everything new; they really didn't know what they were doing. But they learned. Could you do it? I couldn't. But they did—and they did again and again. And it's 2017 and they're still doing it. Go figure.

"It's more than you, it is more than me; Whatever dreams we have they're for the family. We're not alone anymore now there are others there, And that dream's big enough for all of us to share." *Dreamgirls:* **Henry Krieger, Tom Eyen.**

Cocktail waiters were hired. One of the employees even went out and bought a new GMC Pacer. His older brother, who was putting up sheetrock for Robert Martin, wasn't happy, so Jimmy (the employee in question) asked if it would be okay if his older brother could come in for an interview. Dust was flying off him. Bill told younger brother that older brother should really "come in for an interview in a jacket and tie." And so it happened. And older brother also was hired.

As it is said:

"This is the moment, this is the day, when I send all my doubts and demons on their way. Ev'ry endeavour, I have made ever is coming into play, is here and now, today. This is the moment, this is the time, when the momentum and the moment are in rhyme. Give me this moment, this precious chance. I'll gather up my past and make some sense at last." *Jekyll and Hyde:* **Leslie Bricusse and Frank Wildhorn**

SCENE SIX:
IF I HAD MY DRUTHERS

Let's see. The theatre opened in 1974. Let's take a tour of Broadway memory lane and of the shows the Stutlers and Mr. Funking produced since that opening: *Kiss Me Kate; Barefoot in the Park; Guys and Dolls; The Fantastiks; Blithe Spirit; Play It Again, Sam; Tom Jones; Nice Faces of 1943; I Do! I Do!; Man of La Mancha; Oklahoma!; Pajama Game; Bells Are Ringing; South Pacific; Anything Goes; Damn Yankees; Annie Get Your Gun; Carousel; Can-Can; The Sound of Music; George M!; Camelot; Li'l Abner.* The year is now 1977. This new show, *L'il Abner,* will run from July to September. But—wait! Events in the country!

From the newspaper: "Dogpatch to Aid Victims of Flood. An Evening Dinner Theatre in Elmsford, in association with the Westchester Chapter of the American Red Cross, has designated its Aug. 9 performance of 'Li'l Abner' as a special benefit for financial aid to the flood victims of Johnstown, Pa.

"The dinner theater is donating its personnel, food, show and beverages. All sales proceeds will be turned over to the Red Cross and will be sent directly to the flood victims. Damage to that area in Pennsylvania is estimated at over $200 million, with more than 58 known dead and hundreds injured and homeless.

"Tickets are 100 per cent deductible and those who cannot attend but wish to make a contribution may send donations to An Evening Dinner Theatre, made payable to the Red Cross-Food, Theatre at 11 Clearbrook Rd., Elmsford.

"Doors open Aug. 9 at 6:15 p.m. for cocktails with dinner at 7 p.m. and show time at 8:20 p.m. The box office is open daily from noon to 10 p.m. and reservations are accepted by telephone."

Can you imagine any Broadway producer donating a whole performance (food, drinks, and tickets) to *charity*!!!? Neither can I. But the family of producers at An Evening Dinner Theatre did just that.

And members of the press were equally enthusiastic with the caliber of shows put upon the stage of An Evening Dinner Theatre. Take the words of *The Journal America Newspaper,* George & Stacey Malmgren, editors and publishers:

"Over the River and Through the Woods to Westchester Theatre we go, we get lost every time, but we make it on time for every wonderful show! The food is to die for, the shows we all thrive for! The best date night that I know! Every time we walk in, we're met with such big grins; and we feel right at home for the show. The decor is amazing, and changes with seasons and is always excited to go. We've seen so many shows; can't say which is best: They are all great, ya know! I've seen it rain on stage and seen it snow, there's always miracles at these shows! The staff is amazing, and helpful and kind.

"They go out of their way to make sure you're just fine. You leave with your heart always filled with joy from the love that each production has come together to make you applaud!"

The year: 1978. An Evening Dinner Theatre has been in existence for four years. We've seen, right after *L'il Abner, Gypsy, Showboat, Fiddler on the Roof,* and now, *Shenandoah.* It is May.

Ron Holgate stars. He has won a Tony Award, Best Featured Actor in a Musical, for *1776,* and then repeated the same role in the movie. As critic Walter Kerr commented about him, "There is simply no stopping Mr. Holgate as he explodes with the sheer happiness of having come to exist."

53

He appeared on Broadway in *Lend Me a Tenor,* *Annie Get Your Gun* (revival), and toured in the musical *Urinetown.* My wife and I saw him in *The Grand Tour,* starring Joel Grey—a musical that closed, alas, as a failure. My wife and I treated her beloved grandmother—we called her Baba Dear—to this wonderful show; the only Broadway show we would all attend together.

And Ron Holgate appeared at An Evening Dinner Theatre.

Don't forget that Holland Taylor was in *Blithe Spirit!* You know her because you just saw her in *The Front Page* on Broadway. Holland appeared in many Broadway shows, and was nominated for a Tony in a play she wrote about Ann Richards, titled *Ann.* I'm sure you saw her on television where she won a 1999 Emmy for Outstanding Supporting Actress in a Drama Series, *The Practice.* She also appeared on television in *Two and a Half Men.* Just name-dropping . . .

And time marches on . . . *Pippin, West Side Story,* and then *The Music Man.* From November 1978, it ran until February of 1979. It starred: Tom Urich. He appeared at An Evening Dinner Theatre, and also on television: *The Edge of Night.* He also appeared in *Murder at 1600,* and *The Liars' Club.*

Susan Bigelow starred as Marian the Librarian in *The Music Man,* and she appeared in *Wild and Wooly, Face,* and *The Rock Rainbow.*

The Mayor was played by noted actor Willard Waterman. We recognize him from his appearances in the movies *The Apartment, Auntie Mame,* and on television in (for those old enough to remember) *The Great Gildersleeve.*

No, Mr. Bill Stutler did not twirl a baton as part of this show! *Funny Girl* played at An Evening Dinner Theatre from January 1978 through April of 1978. The role of Fanny Brice was played by Rosalind Harris. You probably remember her from the movie *Fiddler on the Roof*. She played the role of Tzeitel, though she had toured the country playing the part of Golde. As you also probably remember, the part of Tevye was played by the noted Israeli actor Topol.

"Don't tell me not to fly. I've simply got to. If someone takes a spill, it's me and not you. Don't bring around a cloud to rain on my parade." *Funny Girl*: **Bob Merrill and Jule Styne.**

Five years. Would you believe it? Three hundred and sixty-five days a year; fifty-two weeks a year. Musical theatre in Westchester, only twenty-five minutes away from Broadway. It's a wonder, here in 1979. The month is May; the month is June; the month is July 1979. Five-year anniversary. What do you think the most perfect show to revisit would be? Of course!

"Brush up your Shakespeare! Start quoting him now. Brush up your Shakespeare! And the women you will wow!" *Kiss Me, Kate:* **Cole Porter.**

Another article—another rave! In an article by Joann Undercoffler, it states the producers had invested much time, much energy, much love, and much money in seeking to give Westchester the best kind of musical theatre possible. We know they succeeded.

The aforementioned Kurt Peterson starred. Vickie Patek played opposite him. She appeared in *Do You Remember Love*; *Broken Promises; Taking Emily Back*; and *The Killing Mind* on television.

Success! An Evening Dinner Theatre is a success!

And *Cabaret* follows in July of 1979, running through to September. In the cast: the late Richard Caspar, as the MC; and Jana Robbins, as Sally Bowles. It is directed and choreographed by Flint Hamblin. From *The New York Times,* August 8, 1990:

"Robert W. (Richard) Casper, an actor, director and choreographer who worked on 30 productions for An Evening Dinner Theater in Elmsford, N.Y., died Friday at Memorial Hospital in Mount Holly, N.J. He was 41 years old and lived in Manhattan. Mr. Casper's sister, Ann G. Zielinski of Lawrenceville, N.J., said the cause of death was pancreatitis.

"Casper, whose professional name was Richard Casper, performed in the dinner theater's first pro-duction, "Kiss Me Kate," in 1974. Later he staged, among other shows, "Dreamgirls," ""Big River," "My Fair Lady" and "My One and Only," which he also directed on a national tour. He directed productions of "Peter Pan" and "Joseph and the Amazing Technicolor Dreamcoat."

"Mr. Casper, who was a graduate of Northwestern University, also directed plays and musicals for the Equity Library Theater, the St. Louis Municipal Opera, the Pittsburgh Civic Light Opera, the Lincolnshire The-ater in Chicago and the Brunswick Musical Theater in Brunswick, Me."

My wife and I saw Jana Robbins, who was the understudy for Mama Rose in a production of *Gypsy*, years ago. She was better in the part than the lead. Jana Robbins appeared in *The Women*; *The Last Days of Frankie the Fly*, and *Executive Target* as well as many touring performances. Incidentally, Ruth Gottschall, a member of the cast, also appeared in the movies: *Annie*; *Everyone Says I Love You*, and *Brother*.

The Unsinkable Molly Brown followed, as did *Same Time, Next Year*. We are now in October of 1979. Star-ring in *Same Time, Next Year* is Betsy Palmer and Tom Troupe. Now that is the same Betsy Palmer who was in the movie *Mr. Roberts*, and the movie *The Long Gray Line*. She was a news reporter on the television news show *Today*, and remained in television . . . like game shows.

Tom Troupe, an actor and writer, appeared in the movies *My Own Private Idaho*, *Kelly's Heroes*, and *Summer School*.

It takes a village . . . and that village is Elmsford, New York. And it takes producers who are in business to make that village a family. The Stutlers and Mr. Funking have achieved that.

Look at all the celebrities who have graced their business—their theatre. Each time we trip down memory lane, we discover another thespian, or director, or choreographer, or stagehand, or stage manager, or lighting director, or musical director who wet their chops in Elmsford—at An Evening Dinner Theatre—and then went on to a celebrated career.

Hello, Dolly (November 1979–February 1980) starred Dorothy Collins. See what I mean? Dorothy Collins appeared on television as the lead singer on *Your Hit Parade*, as well as on *Candid Camera*. She starred in the original cast of Stephen Sondheim's *Follies* and was nominated for a Tony.

What regional theatre do you know of that can boast of such talent? This is Equity talent—vouched for by that union—and certified to be exceptional. Many dinner theatres today feature shows—but they are subcaliber. An Evening Dinner Theatre was anything but. Memory lane: *So Long Stanley; Chicago, Applause, Sweet Charity, Grease, Guys and Dolls* (again), and the year 1980 is over. The theatre still runs fifty-two weeks each year.

"What is it that we're living for? Applause, applause! Nothing I know brings on the glow like sweet applause." *Applause*: **Lee Adams, Charles Strouse**

Please check out the article. It is titled "The price is right," and it's from 1980. And if you will come with me for a bit down the yellow brick road and find yourself with me in 2017, the price is *still* right!

THE PRICE IS RIGHT
by Elaine Russell

The man was bitterly bemoaning the cost of an evening in New York to celebrate his wife's birthday..

"$10 to $15 for a babysitter, then an additional $30 or $40 for dinner, $7 or $8 for parking the car, and anywhere from $18 to $26 for theater tickets. Do you realize that's a minimum of about $90?" he said, a look of shock on his face.

What the man perhaps didn't know was that for less than $50, with babysitter fee included, he could have taken his wife to An Evening Dinner Theatre in the center of Westchester County in Elmsford and enjoyed dinner and a Broadway-quality show.

"People say, 'Yes, but it's not Broadway,'" said Bob Funking, Executive Vice President of An Evening Dinner Theatre. "But that's where they're wrong. It IS Broadway quality, the same directors, the same talent on stage, except the stars. And how many productions on Broadway have stars? A Broadway production often creates a star, but not that many musicals have stars heading the casts."

"The same performers who are working now at An Evening Dinner Theatre will probably move into a Broadway show when the current show finishes its run," said Bill Stutler, President of the theatre.

"Two of the biggest hits on Broadway, 'A Chorus Line' and 'Annie,' don't have stars," Stutler said.

"But we have Mitzi Hamilton for our new production of 'Sweet Charity' opening Wednesday night," Funking said, "And she's leaving 'Chorus Line' to do this show. In fact, she's the one they send out to open every production of 'Chorus Line,' no matter where it is."

And that's star quality, no matter how you look at it. All that, and dinner, too!

The aforementioned Mitzi Hamilton, from *A Chorus Line* headlined their next show, *Sweet Charity*, which played in the summer of 1980. Ms. Hamilton portrayed Val (as the first replacement) in the first production of *A Chorus Line.* She also appeared in *King of Hearts, Seesaw,* and *Pippin.*

Let's stroll down memory lane once more. Following *Sweet Charity* was *Grease, Guys and Dolls* (The producers must really liked this show!), *Shenandoah, No, No, Nanette, and Oliver!* from April 1981 to July of 1981. Faith Prince (of many Broadway shows, including a revival of *Guys and Dolls* with Nathan Lane, was also in *Shenandoah.*

The producers figured that since, at its inception, some in the community expected a bawdy theatre, filled with strippers and lots of sex, they figured *Tom Jones* in the summer of 1981 was a great choice for theatre audiences in Westchester.

The show provided an uplift, a change from the staid Broadway musical ware that had been the foundation of An Evening Dinner Theatre. Kristen Blodgette was the musical director at this show. She has graduated now, in 2017, to a more important role: she is the musical director for Andrew Lloyd Webber. *Cats!* is hers; and . . . *Phantom of the Opera; Sunset Boulevard; Riverdance; Jesus Christ, Superstar; Chitty Chitty Bang Bang, Woman in White, Mary Poppins, Little Night Music* and *Evita.* You might say—and you should say—that she came from a great beginning at An Evening Dinner Theatre and today is, obviously, *somebody in theatre!*

Thank you, Bob Funking and Bill Stutler. Thank you.

Following this smash hit, An Evening Dinner Theatre produced *Baggy Pants Review, I Love My Wife, Meet Me in St. Louis*, and *The Roaring Twenties. I Love My Wife* starred Charles Repole. I know you have heard that name before. Charles Repole, the actor, the director—who first started directing—you guessed it—at An Evening Dinner Theatre! I'll let him tell you: "Bill knew me from Broadway stuff. We didn't meet before that. He had asked me to do *I Love My Wife* at An Evening. I had done it on a national tour. I said, 'Yea, I will!'

"I performed and met him there. We became fast friends. Scott Bakula was in it. We had a ball doing it. Bill asked me if I would direct. First time in my life! I said *okay*! We did *They're Playing Our Song* with Walter Bobbie and Randi Graff.

"It was my first beginning at directing. Never before. Always wanted to. He was so nice. I had been around for a while. There, I was treated with enormous respect. It was spectacular, wonderful. I even learned how to play bridge—during the long intermissions I played bridge! Then we had only two musicians. Later on, I directed for Bill and Bob, *South Pacific, Gypsy, Anything Goes, A Day in Hollywood / A Night in the Ukraine*. It felt like I was directing hundreds of them. I took my directing ability—learned at An Evening Dinner Theatre—to Broadway. I directed on Broadway after all this. Bill Stutler started it! I went from stock . . . finally Broadway. I have worked at City Center. Now I am a college professor, at Queens College. I have been chairman for eight years.

"You know, I was nominated for *Very Good Eddie* for a Tony, for acting. Boy, I am lucky to get everything all in and have a real career.

"At An Evening Dinner Theatre, I found that the best thing is they treat you with great respect . . . it is great fun . . . the audience right there in your face!

"Let me tell you a story. I did *A Day in Hollywood / A Night in the Ukraine*. Vicki Lewis was the star. We are watching—Bill and I are watching—the show in performance prior to opening. At the intermission the stage manager says, 'Vicki is sick and has to go to the hospital.' I went backstage, and sitting with the Harpo wig was her understudy. She was crying. 'What can I do? I don't know the words or the blocking!'

"I put on the Harpo wig, coat, and horn and played the part. I knew all the blocking! Von Ann and Bill laughed. I performed the show. I became the official understudy. I wasn't scared . . . I had to blow my horn, jump on tables . . . actors were happy and laughed! They trusted me!

"Being part of An Evening Dinner Theatre's family was wonderful."

Mr. Repole mentioned other shows that followed *Tom Jones.* redux, 1981-82: *The Roaring Twenties; Fabulous Forties; I Do! I Do!; 1776; Ain't Misbehavin'; Pirates of Penzance; Barnum,* then in January of 1983: *They're Playing Our Song; The Best Little Whorehouse in Texas; Annie, Cabaret . . . A Day in Hollywood / A Night in the Ukraine:* 1984.

The aforementioned Vicki Lewis has a large pedigree. She starred on Broadway in *Chicago;* was in *Damn Yankees, Pal Joey,* and *The Crucible.* She was a soloist at Carnegie Hall. You can hear her voice in the animated *Finding Nemo; Justice League,* and *Phineas and Ferb.* She has been a star on television, including *Curb Your Enthusiasm,* and *Gray's Anatomy.*

Mr. Repole also mentioned Walter Bobbie. Please remember that all these folks began or learned their craft because of a theatre that was a dream of Von Ann and Bill Stutler and Bob Funking. It is called An Evening Dinner Theatre, in Elmsford, New York. Now, Mr. Bobbie: Mr. Bobbie won a Laurence Olivier Theatre Award for his direction of the 1997 *Chicago.* He also won the Tony—Best Director. He has been nominated for Best Book (Musical) for the revival of *Chicago.* He is also a renowned actor.

Randy Graff won a 1990 Tony Award as Best Actress, Featured Role, for *City of Angels.* She was also nominated as Best Actress, Musical, for *A Class Act.* My wife and I saw her when we saw the original production of *Les Miserables.* She originated the role of Fantine and sang (for posterity!) the song "I Dreamed a Dream." She remembers her experience at At Evening Dinner Theatre with fondness.

"I dreamed a dream in days gone by, when hope was high and life worth living. I dreamed that love would never die. I dreamed that God would be forgiving. Then I was young and unafraid and dreams were made and used and wasted. There was no ransom to be paid, no song unsung, no wine untasted." *Les Miserables***: Claude Michel Schonberg, Alain Boubil, Jean-Marc Natel, Herbert Kretzmer.**

SCENE SEVEN:
ONCE YOU LOSE YOUR HEART

L et us please not forget Von Ann Stutler. She is a very important part of the producers' productions.

In an article in *Women's News* from June of 1984, Harriet
Morrison wrote:

> *Von Anne Stutler, co-owner of An Evening Dinner*
> *Theatre in Elmsford, is a prime example of the old adage,*
> *"There's no business like show business." Ms. Stutler, who*
> *has operated the highly acclaimed entertainment arena*
> *with her husband, Bill, and their partner, Bob Funking,*
> *since 1974, established the theatre as an alternative for*
> *a heterogeneous group of suburbanites who would not*
> *necessarily venture to Broadway but could be tapped for*
> *an affordable, enjoyable evening close to home.*
>
> *When she is asked routinely how the theatre got*
> *started, Ms. Stutler quips, "Ignorance and guts." Actu-*
> *ally, the theatre is a tribute to the collaborative skills,*
> *energy and fortitude of its owners. Ms. Stutler's contri-*
> *butions are vital and specific and have grown with the*
> *blossoming of the theatre itself.*
>
> *In July 1974, when the theatre mounted its first*
> *production,* Kiss Me, Kate, *Ms. Stutler was training*
> *staff, selecting silver, glassware and accoutrements, and*
> *running the box office out of her home. As she describes*
> *herself, she was "the doer. We had to sell ourselves, our*
> *energy, our enthusiasm. We had to convince people to*
> *try something new."*
>
> *Ms. Stutler's expanded role at the theatre is a syn-*
> *thesis of many of the previous life and work experiences.*

She draws heavily on her social work background, knowledge acquired as a real estate broker, her musical and artistic talents, and a genuine appreciation of people.

Her savvy in public relations has led to her current major focus, group sales and customer contact. Innovations she has spearheaded have served the dual purpose of satisfying public needs and fully utilizing the theatre. The theatre now services senior citizens at matinees, accommodates business meetings, and provides school groups with special sessions that include question-and-answer periods. Additionally, the theatre now offers well-received Ethnic Nights on Mondays and Tuesdays when there are no regular show performances.

The key to Ms. Stutler's success is best described by her own advice. "Stay open to learning things. When the day comes that you can put your job in a box, then it's time to move on. Get the 'buts' out of your vocabulary. The only way you're going to move forward is not to have a 'but' in your head at all, there are none! There's always a way around them, and you've got to have the openness to find it. That's true with any job, it really is!"

You will note in the article that Von Ann recounts the history of An Evening Dinner Theatre, as she says, "as an alternative for a heterogeneous group of suburbanites who would not necessarily venture to Broadway, but could be interested in an affordable, enjoyable evening close to home."

As you are now aware, having read the previous pages of this tome, as she says, the theatre got started on "Ignorance and guts." She continues, in that article, that "The theatre is a tribute to the collaborative skills, energy and fortitude of its owners." Yup.

As the article concludes, she states that, "Sure, you may run into some walls. There's always a way around them, and you've got to have the openness to find it . . . that's true with any job . . . it really is."

An Evening Dinner Theatre: July 1974–February 1991. RIP. But, wait! There will be a rebirth, and we title it Westchester Broadway Theatre.

Returning to An Evening Dinner Theatre, who can forget the shows that graced that stage—the sixty-second show to the eighty-third. I'm gonna write them down, right here, just to see your amazement—then we'll take a look at the careers spawned and lives uplifted by Von Ann and Bill Stutler and Bob Funking, for their flighty venture of 1974 (who knew?) to the vast success of this enterprise: *Joseph and the Amazing Technicolor Dreamcoat; Kismet; Promises, Promises; Can-Can; Baby; Nine; Evita; The King and I; George M!; Sophisticated Ladies; My One and Only; On Your Toes,* and more. They moved for their eighty-fourth show, *A Chorus Line,* but more on that later.

"I don't expect my love affairs to last for long, never fool myself that my dreams will come true. Being used to trouble, I anticipate it, but all the same I hate it, wouldn't you? So what happens now?" *Evita*: **Tim Rice and Andrew Lloyd Webber**

I've talked over and over again how the producers made this business into a family. It isn't just a word—family—it's a way of living for the Stutlers and Bob Funking. For instance . . . take Phil Hall. Today he is a vocal coach and a voice teacher.

"My first experience with an Evening Dinner Theater is that I filled in for someone (maybe Ian Herman) for a musical revue that had Marianne Challis, Dennis Fox, Laurie Gayle Stephenson, Buddy Crutchfield, and Brooks Almy in it. It had a feeling of the musical *Good News,* but I don't believe it was. I did one performance, I believe. Later, when Kristin Blodgette had to leave *Joseph and the Amazing Technicolor Dreamcoat,* I got asked to musical direct there, and I happily accepted.

"I worked for them for a number of shows as musical director: *Joseph and the Amazing Technicolor Dreamcoat, Can-Can, My One and Only, Baby, 42nd Street, Barnum,* and *Sayonara.* I worked with Richard Casper as director for quite a few shows there, as he was resident director. Richard had a seriously salty (perhaps obscene is a better adjective) tongue, but he was great at directing many successful shows for the Stutlers. In the production of *Baby,* I saw a couple of actors fall in love with one another and end up getting married. My *One and Only* ended up being such a good seller; we did a six-month run of that show (almost unheard of). I had a crush on one of the actors in *Barnum* (Russ Thacker) and ended up dating him for a while. He was so darn charismatic in life and on stage. That wry smile of his.

"The Stutlers were as lovely to me as they possibly could be. They were lovely to me then, and every single time I have asked them for their help subsequent to working there, they have bent over backwards to help me. They (along with Bob Funking, although most of my dealings have been with the Stutlers) are some of the nicest people I've ever known in NYC, and also in theater. I loved Lucille Dixon, who was my bass player for almost every single production with her baby bass. She was a lovely human being, and I also enjoyed working with Kenny Ross, who was both a very nice man and a great drummer. Von Ann became very close friends with Byron Nease, who was also a good friend of mine. Byron had one of the most glorious singing voices I've ever heard. I'm so happy they made such a success of the theater.

"They have provided a *lot* of joy and entertainment to the patrons of their theater, and they have given so, so many actors, musical directors, directors, and choreographers work for so many years. They are angels of Broadway. I can't remember the years I was affiliated with the theater. It was a *long* time ago.

"My favorite anecdote is: Charlie Repole was directing *Baby.* We were in tech on Friday evening, and we had gotten to the point in the show where the musical passed through the fall season. Before leaving, Charlie wanted to see the fall leaves (cut out of something like tissue paper) float down before we left for the night. He was quite emphatic about wanting to see it before leaving, so they cued it up and called the cue. Only problem was, the leaves had been weighted with washers, and, like dead pigeons, they fell to the stage with a resounding thud. Charlie's look of anticipation quickly turned to disappointment, but the anticipatory look on his face followed by the thud of the leaves left me howling with glee. I couldn't stop laughing. It was a great life moment—especially for Charlie Repole."

And . . . Bill McCauley: "I worked as an actor for Bill Stutler and Bob Funking from 1978 to 2012. I was also very close friends with their resident director for many years, Richard Casper (we went to Northwestern University together). At An Evening Dinner Theatre (such an odd name!), I appeared in *Applause, Oliver!,* their landmark production of *The Mystery of Edwin Drood,* and *Me & My Girl. M*ost shows had three-month runs, but *Me & My Girl* ran seven months, being extended several times while the new theatre was being built (and delayed). At Westchester Broadway Theatre, I appeared in *Pirates of Penzance,* two productions of *Singin' in the Rain, It's a Wonderful Life, My Fair Lady,* and *Can-Can.*

"Among other aspects of the theatre, you might want to mention is the "Prime Rib Rule." Like theaters everywhere, WBT is subject to the weather, and through the years Elmsford has had its share of blizzards and hurricanes, in which case the actors and staff are phoned and told not to come in to work. The final word in this is the Prime Rib Rule. No matter the weather or the circumstance, if the chef has put the prime rib in the oven for that evening's performance, the show goes *on*. That rule is written in stone.

"An Evening served a beautiful buffet brunch every weekend before the Sunday matinee. After many years, the buffet was discontinued because hungry actors were emptying the tables when they arrived for work.

"I was a working actor for fifty-six years, and for the last several years I have been working for the Shubert Organization, helping to manage the Broadway Theatre."

The people, the stars, the directors, the musicians: Take *Joseph,* for instance. It ran at An Evening from February 1984 to May 1984. It starred Iris Revson, Stephen McDonough, Mark McGrath, Glory Crampton, and was directed by Richard Casper. Yes, that's the same Richard Casper who directed so many shows for the producers. It's the same Richard Casper (he directed and appeared as the MC in *Cabaret*),who directed and choreographed the off-Broadway revival of *The Robber Bridegroom.*

You know he did more than that . . . I have mentioned him previously, prominently!

Iris Revson (who appeared on Broadway in *The Pirates of Penzance* as Merlin, and as Eva Peron in the first national company of *Evita*) starred in Elmsford for the producers. Stephen McDonough was in the Broadway production of *Take Me Along.* Glory Crampton—a very young actress—began at An Evening Dinner Theatre.

More on her fabulous career later.

Baby, directed and choreographed by the aforementioned Charles Repole, featured: Donna Drake (original in *A Chorus Line* on Broadway; Stephen Fenning (*Hair* and *You're A Good Man, Charlie Brown* on Broadway); Mark McGrath (Broadway: *Scarlet Pimpernel, Three Musketeers, Little Me*); David Cantor (*Evita* Broadway understudy.)

Nine here.

Evita, in June of 1985, featured Paige O'Hara and Carolee Carmello for matinees.

I would bet that any Broadway producer today would be ecstatic to have either performer in any one of their plays. As you know, Paige O'Hara was the voice of Belle in the 1991 movie *Beauty and the Beast*. She also appeared on Broadway in *The Mystery of Edwin Drood*, and the revival of *Showboat*.

Carolee Carmello starred in *Urinetown, Mamma Mia,* and won a Drama Desk Award in 1999 for Outstanding Actress in *Parade. S*he also appeared in the AMC television show *Remember WENN*.

Boy! This trip down memory lane is exhausting, isn't it?

"What good is sitting alone in your room? Come hear the music play; Life is a Cabaret, old chum, come to the Cabaret. Put down the knitting, the book and the broom, time for a holiday; Life is a Cabaret, old chum, come to the Cabaret. Come taste the wine, come hear the band, come blow the horn, start celebrating, right this way, your table's waiting, No use permitting some prophet of doom, to wipe ev'ry smile away; Life is a Cabaret, old chum, come to the Cabaret." *Cabaret*: Fred Ebb, John Kander

Let's take pause on our trip down An Evening Dinner Theatre's memory lane. Two individuals who got their nachus and experience with Von Ann and Bill Stutler and Bob Funking are noted individuals in the arts today.

First, there's Scott Bakula. If you watch *NCIS: New Orleans*, he's the star. If you watched *Quantum Leap*, he's the star. If you saw the movie *Star Trek: Enterprise*, that was him. If you saw the award-winning *Behind the Candelabra*, he was in it. He also was nominated for a Tony Award in 1988 for the Broadway show *Romance, Romance*.

To An Evening Dinner Theatre and there, he was helped a lot by Bob Funking. You know why he liked An Evening Dinner Theatre? "You could be as close to New York as that theater was and do a quality production so close to Broadway. It was a great advantage for me and hundreds of actors. People in New York could come to see you. What a job! People who saw you could then talk about you. It was a great opportunity, and you were getting paid. You were working, not as a waiter, not as a busboy. You could live in your own apartment while still doing what you came to New York to do—to be in theatre. The work was great, with a quality of people in shows with spectacular results.

"At first, I auditioned. I wasn't yet established. I had done a few things in the city, like showcases. An Evening Dinner Theatre fit in to some spaces in my schedule. I can't get the experience out of my head! I was in *Grease,* and *I Love My Wife!*

"We were so close to Broadway shows. The shows changed very quickly, and because of my parts at An Evening, I eventually got good connections. Just like the connections Stutler and Funking had! Every recent hit on Broadway, they got the rights and brought it to Elmsford, right in their neighborhood!

"A story: My favorite remembrance was *I Love My Wife.* Charles Repole, the director and an actor in the show, in the second act, where there was a wife-swapping portion, always jumped into bed—the set was made with a pullout bed, from a couch. Meanwhile, Charlie was doing his twenty minutes as a shy, nervous character. He was always spectacular, hysterical. He had come to An Evening right after the revival on Broadway. It's very hard to keep a straight face with Charlie; he was always doing something weird. Anyway, my character was always ready to jump into bed. Shtick things. Then, abruptly *the entire sofa bed* broke! Collapsed onto the floor! We were dying! Randy Graff was under the sheets, laughing so hard! It was perfect for Charlie. It was my favorite horrible moment . . . perfectly timed . . . don't remember what he said, what he did . . . but it was hilarious!

"Working at an Evening Dinner Theatre was wonderful. I'm still happy to be working at my age . . . I especially like being on *Quantum Leap* from 1989 to '93, . . . I kept working. I started with the straw hat summer circuit . . . meeting people

. . . expanding my framework of friends in New York. I did a 1986 musical *Nightclub Confidential*. Then *Romance, Romance* on Broadway. It was a blast being part of An Evening Dinner Theatre, and the family of the Stutlers and Bob Funking."

Next, let's examine Mr. Kurt Peterson. He first got involved with An Evening Dinner Theatre in 1975, when he appeared in *Tom Jones.* He got the part because his agent submitted his resume, and he aced his audition. He appeared at An Evening in *I Do, I Do* twice; *Kiss Me, Kate; Camelot* at Northstage (a theatre the producers opened on Long Island that only had a short existence). He appeared in many special events, like Christmas specials. "The most important show I did was *Side by Side by Sondheim* for a couple of performances. It was directed by Rob Marshall. It was sold to Columbia Artists Management! Because of Stutler and Funking, Columbia Artists saw that production and sent it out on the road!

"Gosh sakes! They (Stutler and Funking) totally allowed me to do roles I wouldn't be able to do anywhere else. It helped pay the rent. An Evening Dinner Theatre was a launching pad for many, many people: choreographers, actors, musicians. I agree that today every Broadway show probably has an alumnus from An Evening Dinner Theatre or Westchester Broadway Theatre. Stutler and Funking do not get enough credit! So many people owe a great deal to these people! They are the sweetest, most generous people in the world. Their generosity—as human beings they are the most generous in the world, personally and professionally.

"My wife and I went up to visit them on Candlewood Lake . . . they mentioned to their realtor . . . the realtor found us a house near them, in Bridgewater. On weekends we have pizza and see them!

"Anyone who has had contact with them is well taken care of; the cast is always well taken care of. They are treated, not like employees, but family.

"Of course, there was a lot of partying. We even travelled together; we went to the Virgin Islands together.

"Today I continue to perform (I have my own voice and production company) just like Bill Stutler and Bog Funking . . . it's called James William Productions.com. I owe them a special debt of gratitude, as does the whole industry."

Just as an aside: In 1977, the late Clark Gesner (composer of *You're a Good Man, Charlie Brown*), asked Kurt to record a demo of a brand-new Christmas song for Bing Crosby. Sadly, Bing passed away just a few weeks before the session. It would be the "last Christmas song Bing never recorded," but now you can hear the lovely "All Kinds of Christmases" sung by Kurt, with orchestrations and piano by Rick Jensen.

So, ladies and gentlemen, you see how Von Ann and Bill Stutler and Bob Funking have spawned a family of performers in the industry, people who have worked in An Evening Dinner Theatre (and then Westchester Broadway Theatre). They have found fame and fortune—but never, ever have forgotten their wonderful experiences in Elmsford. What other producers in our country could possibly make that claim?

SCENE EIGHT: ASK YOUR HEART, WHAT GAVE THE WORLD ITS START

I promised you a tour of the talent in those final shows at An Evening Dinner Theatre before it moved to Westchester Broadway Theatre. I know you are interested in what became of personalities who appeared or worked at the theatre, so . . .

The King and I, which ran November 1985–March 1986, featured Beth Fowler and William Kiehl. Beth Fowler is celebrated for Broadway's *Take Me Along,* and *Baby,* and two Tony nominations for playing Mrs. Potts in *Beauty and the Beast,* and Mrs. Lovett in *Sweeney Todd.* William Kiehl has dubbed 400 films into English and has appeared in *The Edge of Night* on television, among other roles.

Moving on. G*eorge M!* followed. It's the story of George M. Cohan, and it starred Frank Root, from Broadway's *Mack and Mabel.* Root appeared on television on *Boardwalk Empire,* among others.

Memory lane! *Sophisticated Ladies* followed. Then *My One and Only.* Richard Casper directed that, and it stared George Dvorsky and Donna Kane. George Dvorsky's voice appeared in the movies *Beauty and the Beast* in 1991; *Pocahontas* in 1995, and *Mulan* in 1998. He has appeared in many television shows as well. Donna Kane won an Off-Broadway award for Best Actress in *Dames at Sea.* She appeared in *Meet Me in St. Louis* in 1989 and has toured with *Joseph and the Amazing Technicolor Dreamcoat* and *Les Miserables,* among others. Such talent—and all appeared at An Evening Dinner Theatre!

On Your Toes; Sugar Babies; The Mystery of Edwin Drood; La Cage aux Folles; Dreamgirls; My Fair Lady; 42nd Street; Big River; Camelot; Anything Goes, and, finally, the last show at An Evening Dinner Theatre: *Me and My Gal,* August 1990–

February 1991. O*n Your Toes* had been nominated for a Tony; it came straight from Broadway. "Jamie Ross was the first replacement on Broadway, and he came to us. He then went on to television's *Law and Order*.

Some special names: Paige O'Hara, Rebecca Luker (*Edwin Drood*), Paige O'Hara (again) and George Dvorsky (again) in *Anything Goes*, directed by Charles Repole; *My Fair Lady* featured Meg Bussert and Mark Jacoby; right after that show, Jacoby went into Broadway's *Chicago! Camelot* starred Meg Bussert and P.J. Benjamin and Brian Sutherland; James Young, Stephanie Douglas, and William McCauley starred in *Me and My Girl*; it was again directed by Charles Repole.

You know, of course about Paige O'Hara's career. Rebecca Luker went on to Broadway fame in such "minor" shows as *Fun Home, Cinderella, Mary Poppins, Nine, Secret Garden, Showboat, Phantom of the Opera, Music Man*, etc. And she appeared in the chorus at An Evening Dinner Theatre! "She had an incredible voice!" *Sugar Babies* had Alan Sues, from TV's *Laugh-In*, and Wanda Rickert, a known Broadway performer, was also at An Evening. Bob Arnold—who was there then, too, got a Broadway show and left.

Meg Bussert, you must remember (if you are a Broadway fan) from *The Music Man* (with Dick Van Dyke), *Brigadoon, Irene,* and a tour of *Camelot. S*he was also nominated for a Tony in 1981.

P.J. Benjamin has to his credits *Torch Song Trilogy,* and *Long Day's Journey Into Night.* Mark Jacoby, even though he periodically returns to Elmsford, originated the part of the Phantom in Broadway's *Phantom of the Opera. Y*ou might have seen him on the Great White Way in one of these shows: *Man of La Mancha; Showboat; Ragtime; Sweeney Todd*, and a tour of *Wicked. N*ow you're probably saying to yourselves that Stutler and Funking really created a nurturing group, a showplace for many of Broadway's (and television's and the movies') talent! And you're probably right!

In 2014 (to skip ahead a bit) there was an interview given by Bill Stutler and Bob Funking on a cable link, sponsored by

Pennysaver. It was called "Frank talks with Bruce the Blog." That interview reviewed the past forty years of theatre in Elmsford by the producers. At that time (three years ago), they had accomplished then what most American producers could not and did not accomplish during their lifetimes. At the time, *Mary Poppins* was the show.

As Bob said, for this interview, this special theatre, "Showcases people in the community, and is a positive influence in the community." The producers reviewed their current show and mentioned that "Mary flies over the audience!" At that time, my eight-year-old grandson marveled at how that could be done! Most theatregoers marveled also!

The producers reviewed their history. "They found an ad business that looks interesting. Von Ann and Bill talked to Bob, who was a gourmet cook and had a theatrical background." He was interested. The producers mentioned that in 1974, there were ninety-six Equity theatres in the United States and that dinner theatre was a very big portion of Equity money. In 2017, there are only seven left, Equity and a few nonunion.

The producers attributed this to the rise of the Internet, cable, and the many TV channels. "When they started in 1974, there were only three major channels. Contrast that to today!" As the producers said in that interview, it is a "testament to their longevity, for they are definitely one of the rare breed in theatre!"

"It's gotten harder today," according to Bob. "The audience has so many outlets for entertainment because of technology and the digital world. Everybody wants instant gratification!"

"In 1974, there was a code for theatre: evening dress for women, men wore jackets." Bob continued, "They don't let you in today unless you have a hole in your jeans!" Today's audiences show a terrible lack of etiquette. "Today people come in shorts and flip-flops!"

Both producers lauded the quality of food at the Westchester Broadway Theatre, for "the quality of the food is very important, the menu is generous, great value, no sandwiches." They had their own kitchens with cooked food.

They remembered the designing of Westchester Broadway Theatre—more on that soon—and Judith Chafee designed Westchester Broadway Theatre with seven levels, no bad seats, swivel chairs. You see, people, in Elmsford, "The comfort level helped them survive all these years." Stutler and Funking mentioned in this *Pennysaver* interview that at the new theatre, there is an "Intimate seating; no seats are blocked. There is an intimate close up because of the thrust stage." Years before, An Evening Dinner Theatre featured concerts with Tom Jones, Harry Belafonte, George Carlin, and many others. There were comedy nights to ethnic nights. "You name it, we done it—King Brodeur (agent) provided the town! If you wanted a flea market, he provided you with whatever you wanted. If you wanted a Pavarotti—you got a Pavarotti.'

They mentioned that in the past forty years at An Evening Dinner Theatre and then at the Westchester Broadway Theatre, there was always a Broadway caliber of director and actors. For instance, "Estelle Harris, who played George's mother in *Seinfeld*, told them that they would never pay her enough! She always complained."

Holland Taylor appeared in *Blithe Spirit,* and Susan Waldman. Yes, Susan Waldman, who is now a Yankees announcer, has appeared as an actress in some shows. *Nine* was the last show before she joined the Yankees. In that show, the star, George AAA refused to drink. His mother and brother sat with Bob and Bill during the show. At the vitriolic stuff on stage, his mother remarked, 'That is George!'"

Bob Funking was responsible for contracts of various special nights they had at the theatre(s). There was always a Hamilton High School graduation, where the kids are all dressed up. They did it gratis, and had been doing it for many years.

They've had weddings at their theatres, even one where a bride and groom popped out of the stage!

You can see that many people stayed with them for many years—they actually seem to have had a family plan! It has been related that one time, someone on stage (he shouldn't have been!) fell in the pit. It was an agent! He shouldn't have been onstage in the first place!

It's easy to say, "There's nothing like live theater. These Broadway expenses are crazy!" Two thirds of all Broadway audiences are tourists.

The interview at that time concluded with a truth from then to now: "WBT is the longest-running Equity theater of fifty-two weeks a year in the country."

Since you all know now what I've discovered—that the Stutlers and Bob Funking have set up a unique business in musical theatre that encompasses a huge family, let's visit with one person. Meet Sue Katz, from Westco Productions, who has produced many children's shows, and now is the matinee manager for Westchester Broadway Theatre.

"I started in the late seventies. I was with Westco Productions. I worked with Bill and Bob from that old theatre, initially Monday and Tuesday nights. There were special shows that wouldn't sustain a long run, like.*Godspell, Hair, Pippin,* and *Jesus Christ Superstar.*

"I originally met Bob and Bill through a contact on the national tour of *Godspell* who knew them. 'I want you to meet these guys . . . they just opened a dinner theatre.' He was a mutual friend.

"I worked at Westco theatre for young audiences. My home base is in White Plains. I started doing shows at An Evening Dinner Theatre, fairy tales like *Frosty, the Snowman*, and original Christmas productions. At one time we had four shows on Saturday: nine, eleven, one and three! It was the wonderful 1980s!

"My work at Westco involved me working a lot elsewhere. I worked that full-time job for thirty years. Mayor Al Delvecchio wanted cultural productions, pops in the park . . . different things cultural for the recreation department.

"I finally retired in 2010 and decided that after a year and a half I didn't want to sit home. Bob and Bill were looking for a matinee house manager. 'Sure, I'd like to do it!' P.S., *I am doing that!* I'm working on sponsorships like Pepsi . . . with senior living homes . . . theatre is hard these days. We're trying to capture an audience that can't afford to go into Manhattan.

Years ago, when there was An Evening Dinner Theatre, we were so close–before competitive prices got crazy on Broadway. And we had Broadway-caliber talent! Now we're trying to capture theatre-going audiences . . . we really want to stay local . . . we have a dinner show . . . we have matinees for senior groups. We are trying to find younger people trying to grab on to theatre. Millennials. Our concerts are packed . . . people today are particular for what to choose.

"We have Broadway-caliber shows in Elmsford; always have.

"Take Kristen Blodgette, from our own An Evening Dinner Theatre. Music director here. Now she's Andrew Lloyd Webber's personal assistant. You see *Cats* revived today on Broadway? That's her. She started—she started at An Evening Dinner Theatre!

"As for myself, I have gone along the way. Once I worked on the buffet line; now I'm in an administrative position. I am truly one of the old-time people. People don't realize how much work goes in to making it the success it is. I have been a house manager: trying to keep every department going—even the kitchens, bathrooms. Here everybody is dedicated. Bill Stutler and Bob Funking really give people the opportunity to work . . . to advance . . . they are very empathetic . . . they are caring about people . . . the evolution of this theatre is that unique coming along the way. There is much history on the walls . . ."

You see what I mean? Everyone who has been affiliated with Stutler and Funking, from a waitress to a musical director, feels that they have been part of a family.

Oh! Here's a story! A true story! Yul Brynner's friend Rusty Thacker was playing the lead in *George M!* They had been in a flop show together previously. So Yul Brynner called and said he wanted to come incognito. He decided to come up by helicopter. The copter landed in Robert Martin's parking crossover. Von Ann went to greet Yul in a small car and was greeted instead by a policeman. The policeman inquired as to what was going on! Then the helicopter landed! Surprise! Yul Brynner, incognito, with wife and pilot and bodyguard were squeezed the three blocks to the theatre. The policeman let them go. Yul Brynner was easily recognized.

He and his entourage ended up at a corner table where he then ordered a bottle of vodka. Some in the audience thought that Kojak had landed! It wasn't Telly Savalas—it was Yul. After the show, he signed autographs!

"Give my regards to Broadway, remember me to Herald Square; tell all the gang at Forty-Second Street that I will soon be there. Whisper of how I'm yearning to mingle with the old-time throng; Give my regards to Broadway and say that I'll be there, 'ere long. *GEORGE M!* **music and lyrics by George M. Cohan**

Did I mention Glory Crampton—erstwhile partner in theatre to Robert Cuccioli? Yes, ladies and gentlemen, she began her career as an ingénue—at the age of eighteen!

"I auditioned for the chorus of *Joseph and the Amazing Technicolor Dreamcoat.* I didn't even know what an audition was! A friend took me to audition and sat with me and hundreds of girls. I then entered a room and heard bars of music . . . I was really green! I got the part and my Equity card from doing that job.

"Back then, there was a buffet. All actors were allowed to go through the buffet as many times as you wanted. There was great food, great fresh cookies. Most actors took cookies back to the dressing rooms! A lot of people worked back then. We were allowed to take two bottles of beer before each show. Then at the end of the show we were permitted to take out a bottle of beer. It was the coolest thing, especially for someone like me, just out of college.

"Even after I graduated college . . . throughout my career, I went back. I starred as *Gigi*. Robert Johanson from the Paper Mill Playhouse saw me, and he cast me to do *Gigi* at Paper Mill, where there were twelve leading ladies.

"The important show *Phantom of the Opera*—not the Andrew Lloyd Webber one—originally opened in Houston.

Westchester Broadway Theatre was the first place it was done regionally. I knew Bob Cuccioli before, from *Jekyll And Hyde.* I remember when he broke his leg. On stage, Jim Gertz mouthed the words, while Bob, in the upstairs booth, did all the singing! Then, opening week, I lost my voice . . . my understudy went on. Hard to put on a show with leads out!

"Can-Can was the last show when I worked there. I also appeared in *Nine,* which was an incredible production . . . Bob Cuccioli starred . . . I was Luisa . . .

"Family at Westchester Broadway Theatre was the key . . . Bill and Bob always considered the people who worked for them as special. They are the nicest people. Bill really cares about his shows. Loves his theatre. Lisa Tiso (an associate producer today) started when she was a kid!

"Wonderful memories."

She mentioned Lisa Tiso, who is now the associate producer. Let's see, Lisa started in December 1979 as a buffet girl. Buffet ended in 1981, and we started serving meals. At the new building, we only served meals—except on Thanksgiving.

Let's take a fast segue to the new building . . . Westchester Broadway Theatre.

It is now 1981 . . .

ENTRE-ACT: INTERMISSION

We humbly ask our readers to take a half-hour intermission from reading this book to visit the lounge areas, the gift shop, or to partake in our between-show varieties of special drinks and desserts.

While you are waiting for Act II, may I mention the many . . .

FAMILIES THAT WORKED AT WBT

Jumper: Jimmy, Robert, Mike, Matt, Chris, Tommy
Leslie Davis: Kim and Kathy
Lifieri: Bruce, Jeff, Barry
Tucker: Matt and John (Karon) kid
Taggert: Jeannie (Calleran) Ann, Mary, Leo; children: Kaitlyn and Brynne
Marrero: Katy and Lilia
Santangelo: Chris, Jenny, Beth
Kennedy: Kevin, Billy
Williams: Barbara, Christina
Tiso: Lisa, Chris, Arlene, Mary; children: Carmen and Kimberly
Michaud: Pat, Mike, Joe
Dolans: Maureen, Brendan, Terry, Deirdra, Shawn
Buckley: Christina
Papadardo: Rachel, Michelle, Nick
Mazzuolo: Penny, Renda
McMahon: Kathleen, Susan, Elissa
O'Dell: Regina, Katherine, Caroline
DeRosa; Matt, T Marcie, Lauren
Lovino: Gina, Mike

Oliva: Paul, Paulette (Paul is now the Mt. Pleasant police chief)
Esposito: Giancarlo, Vinnie
Richard King/Rick King: Bob's brother and nephew
Kramer: Brian, GM
McKee: Jimmy, Terry, Peter
Raicis: Scott, Mike
Mosca: Ann Marie, Chris, Elaine

Conciator: Liz, Joe

And the . . .

MARRIAGES OF PEOPLE WHO WORKED FOR THE STUTLERS AND BOB FUNKING

Ryan Stutler/Renee Rappa
Mark McGrath/Lynn Witnersoreor (actors)
Gene Belrans/Lydida Meliore
Steve Callarhan/Jeanie Taggart
Rick King/Audry Aquaviva
Jim McKoo/Holly Washluck
Leo Taggart/Ginny Santianato (divorced)
Nick Pappalardo/Julie Lloyd
Phil Roccuzzo/Melissa Polzer
Jeff Lifrien/Judy Cappello
Heidi Giarlo: group sales manager
Ron Schlighting: box office manager
Alex Sampaio: chef
Ann Marie Mosca: Ass't dining room manager
Rana Attia: crew chief/wardrobe mistress
Viktor Lucas: production stage manager

ACT II
WESTCHESTER
BROADWAY THEATRE

SCENE ONE: GIVE ME SOMEBODY TO DANCE FOR, GIVE ME SOMEBODY TO SHOW

We begin this scene with Associate Producer Lisa Tiso: "In February of 1991, we moved into the new building. I became the assistant box office manager, then I managed food sales.

"In 1989, the new building started being a possibility. We had no room. No stage room, no room for costumes, sets, actors. Even the main offices had to be moved across the street. As the administrative assistant, I helped organize everything with new plans, new building.

"They moved because things were going very well. Theatrically, we ran out of things theatrically we could do. That space was too small in the way of the productions.

"They were looking for another space to build where there could be more luxury boxes There is a Burt Reynolds Theatre in Florida with luxury boxes. Bob and Bill wanted them for their new theatre.

"The 1980s was the best decade, as I like to say. In general, we had outgrown that space. As I mentioned, the offices were across the street. Now the old building is a play place.

"I worked as a director eventually. When we moved into this building, David Cunningham and I worked very close together . . . I was an associate producer at the time. In 1992 I became the other associate producer. Bill went to Mexico on vacation. *Gigi* was the first show David and I produced, with Bill/Bob as executive producers. In February was the show we produced. Dave and I handled it together. Then Dave retired. I like to laugh because I have the largest office . . . Originally it was for four people . . . all gone. No one left, only me.

"When Bill and Bob went on vacation, I was in charge. Pretty much today, now, I produce the shows as their executive. For instance, Bill will be in Mexico in January. We have to choose a cast for *Mamma Mia*. At this point, I've obviously learned all I know. I'm in charge."

And Lisa Tiso was!

Fast-forward a bit in the history of Westchester Broadway Theatre. Lisa?

"It was Superstorm Sandy. We were doing *Fiddler on the Roof*; it was very heartwarming. The Wednesday matinee, luckily, we had electricity; we had only lost it for twenty-four hours. Dedication! Every single cast member from Englewood, New Jersey, New York City, everywhere, came to appear in the show. One actor got online at five in the morning and hired a black car to get over the bridge to perform for our customers. We didn't make anybody come. Over three hundred people came for the matinee in that horrible storm! Amazing dedication from our crew, our actors, and our audience!

"I have dealt, and I deal directly with actors. I like to think of all the good things, like the dedication shown for our *Fiddler*. I personally didn't have electricity for seven days. It was remarkable what the actors did to get here. I wrote letters to each and every actor. I was so incredibly touched that they worked so hard to get here for the show during Superstorm Sandy!

"Everybody who has appeared here or worked here calls it a family. I remember when Cuccioli and Glory Crampton did *Phantom/Jekyll Hyde* together. I always wanted to have Cuccioli and Crampton play Guido and Luisa ever since I met them. It is funny that they both appeared together on Broadway and Off-Broadway in *The Rothschilds* and *Nine*. *Nine is* my all-time favorite musical ever (also Bill's).

"When Westchester Broadway Theatre was built, there was a traditional orchestra pit in 1990. It was then moved to upstairs because a turntable was built center stage for *Phantom*. *Cats* extended out to the tables, and we built a crawl space in there. We also had screens . . . today they serve for advertising. They're also good for the graduations we do. We tried with screens for Alexander Hamilton's High School graduation. We have a live feed on screens. We have it, and it's appealing to people. We do it because it's a local Elmsford school, and we do a lot for the community.

"*Gigi*, in February 1995, was my first show produced. All shows that followed me, I was associated with David. The February shows we exclusively produced. Bill was involved in casting. Now I arrange all the auditions. First we do a breakdown of cast, for agents to submit actors. We run Equity scale. Very few dinner theatres left in the country do.

"For *Singing in the Rain.* My brother-in-law came in and did all the plumbing for the show. The rain for this show was spectacular. Best we ever had. The audience went crazy.

"Our *Phantom* was the best. You would think that if we were able to run a show for nine months, to build up an audience. it had to be good!

"To the show *Chicago* in 2003 . . . usually we request the rights to a show a year in advance. MTI is the worst today. *Chicago* was still running on Broadway, but the Weisslers signed off on it. They let us have the rights. They thought that the show wouldn't be running in 2003, but it was. We, of course, sent the contract and deposit back immediately. The movie was coming out! It was still playing on Broadway, to sold out. The movie was highly successful—Rob Marshall directed. You know, of course, that he directed *A Chorus Line* for us, back in 1991, when we opened the Westchester Broadway Theatre. We sold out. At our first performance of *Chicago,* the producers on Broadway—the Weisslers—got tickets to see the show, to make sure that we didn't steal any stuff from them. It was the first performance; both Bob and Bill were away. It's *Chicago,* everybody's wearing black. After the Weissler's came, we got a certified letter the very next day that we had stolen their logo. We were not entitled to use it. We were wrong. The words were white, within the name. So a labor lawyer writes a lovely letter on our behalf. We ran a whole run of programs. I went to Staples and bought two dozen red markers. We all sat down and colored the white words in red, so we weren't in any jeopardy. The Weisslers couldn't do anything about it. We complied by coloring in the letters on the program. The flyers we threw out. Because the Weisslers signed off prematurely, we couldn't extend *Chicago.* Just goes to show you that our audience doesn't go to Broadway. People who are interested in theatre don't go to Broadway because it's twenty-five miles away. People come to us to spend a whole night out—dinner, free parking, and excellent shows.

"I live in Ardsley, and there are people who don't come here. How can we reach these people? There's got to be a way. Bill's one generation, I'm another. I have a twenty-three-year-old. I was involved in her life. It's a different world today.

"I especially remember Scott Bakula. I was in a teen buffet tunic. In between shows, I spent time on the picnic table talking to him. He was beautiful. I watch his show today. It was beautiful. I love working at Westchester Broadway Theatre.

"Acting at the Westchester Broadway Theatre is very appealing. The actors get to sleep in their own beds. They can keep their survival jobs, their day jobs, and because of the four hundred and forty-nine people of our audience, runs are longer and guaranteed. Actors get their health insurance based on how many weeks they work each year. We helped. There is X amount of weeks of work, which entitles an actor to health benefits. We have had actors who after taxes made more money on unemployment, but, thanks to us, they are getting health insurance. As I said, this is a great family place."

Thank you, Lisa Tiso. She has taken us for a tour of the history of this theatre from when the building was built in 1971 to today. What a ride! Let's check out an article on Lisa from *The Journal News*: The date is November 29, 2014, and it's by Jenny Higgons.

Lisa Tiso Began at the Bottom and Rose to the Top

Jenny Higgons, jhiggons@lohud.com12:00 a.m. ET Nov. 29, 2014

Tiso has many friends who work on Broadway but has no desire to work there herself.

Tiso is the producer of the Westchester Broadway Theatre's current musical, "South Pacific." The Ardsley resident has produced more than 30 main stage musicals at the Westchester Broadway Theatre. She worked her way up from buffet girl to producer. She is much to be complimented on the continued success of Westchester Broadway Theatre in this year of 2017. Her drive, her knowledge, her grit—sustain Bill and Bob!

Lisa Tiso went from feeding the audiences at the Westchester Broadway Theatre to entertaining them. She began as a buffet girl at the community dinner theater in Elmsford in 1979 when she was 15, and since then has produced more than 30 of its main stage musicals. Her current production is "South Pacific," which runs through Sunday, breaks for the holidays, and returns from Dec. 31 through Jan. 25.

"One of my sisters got a job as a buffet girl in 1976," says Tiso, 49, "and then my other sister the year after." Cleaning up the buffet tables after 400 diners had passed through wasn't exactly glamorous, but she did get to hang out with a pre-'Quantum Leap' Scott Bakula when he played the teen angel in the theatre's 1980 "Grease."

"And John Lloyd Young was in our 'Camelot' in 1999,'" she remembers. He went on to win a Tony for playing Frankie Valli in 'Jersey Boys' and then starred in Clint Eastwood's film version.

"As with the many other high schoolers from Valhalla, Hawthorne and Ardsley (where she grew up and still lives) who had after-school jobs there, my main goal was to have a part-time job anywhere, not necessarily in the theater world."

After high school, Tiso took some business classes at Westchester Community College and stayed on at the theatre. When it started offering table-side service, the need for buffet girls decreased, so Tiso grabbed an opportunity to work at the box office instead of waitressing in the dining room. "I loved the box office because there was more interaction with the customers," she says.

We jump to three years later, when Tiso was elevated to a full-time position at the box office. Then, in 1983, she was promoted to assistant box office manager. "Nothing was computerized," she remembers with a laugh. "Everything was done on paper, but I loved it."

Her theatre career continued on the upswing when she was moved into group sales. She made another leap in 1989, when she became the executive assistant to the theatre's longtime executive producers, Bob Funking and Bill Stutler.

In 1991, Funking and Stutler bumped her up to being one of the theatre's three associate producers and then, in 1994, a producer. That promotion got Tiso involved in managing budgets, casting actors, and hiring the stage crew.

Tiso partly attributes her longevity at the theatre to having worked in and worked with its many departments. "Two very different types of businesses operate in our one building," she says, "There are the actors, and then there's everyone else, and one couldn't survive without the other."

Tiso's favorite theatre show has so far been *The Phantom of the Opera* in 1992 because, she says, "After having debuted on Broadway only six years before, it was all so new," and then in *Gigi* in 1994, because it was the first show she fully produced.

Though Elmsford is just a 30-minute drive from The Great White Way, Tiso isn't lured by its bright lights. "Those shows aren't much different from our shows," she says. "Basically, they just have bigger budgets. And *because* we're so close to Manhattan, the talent we can attract is like no other dinner theater. I fell into a job at the Westchester Broadway Theatre, and it turned into a career I love."

Here are 10 things you might not know about Lisa Tiso:

1. Her dog, Maximus, is a cairn terrier.
2. Bruce Springsteen, The Partridge Family, Queen, Led Zeppelin, Jimmy Roselli, Carrie Underwood, Florida Georgia Line, and a few show tunes are on her iPad.
3. She regularly attends the home games of West Point's women's volleyball team.
4. Ocean City, Maryland, is her favorite vacation destination.
5. She's a huge fan of Silvio's Italian Restaurant & Pizzeria in Yonkers.
6. She'd rather be at a Yankees game than a Broadway show.
7. Derek Jeter was her favorite Bronx Bomber.
8. She loves TVs "NCIS" and "Criminal Minds." "Ally McBeal" was her most recent "must-see" TV series.
9. Her parents didn't pick out her first and middle names until a few days after she was born.
10. She has no DVR.

She mentioned another associate producer, David Cunning-ham. Before we figure out how the Stutlers and Bob Funking got to build their own theatre (!), let's see what Mr. Cunningham remembers.

He started in 1975 as a follow spot operator, then he worked through many positions to become stage manager. It is a position he held on to from 1977, on and off for a couple of years.

"In the mid-eighties, after being on the road, I came back as an associate producer. I produced with Lisa. We were both associate producers. First there was me, then she joined. The Stutlers and Bob Funking decided it was time to let us produced shows . . . get our feet wet. With the show *Gigi,* we hired, man-aged the whole show, from auditioning to stage. Lisa hired the director, designers . . .

"The first main show we produced was *Pajama Game* in 1974. I stage managed my first show, *Camelot.* I produced five shows there.

"I left in 2005 because my son went off to college, and I was divorced. I figured it was time to have a midlife crisis. I had started out as a photographer.

"I remember Westchester Broadway Theatre. It wasn't fun every day! For thirty I must have enjoyed it, having a great time. I think working in theatre is always working in crisis moments.

"I remember technical problems. I remember other prob-lems. But there we were all best friends . . . we all have our own personalities . . . it's collaborative. Sometimes there were conflicts. After you're done fixing things, you congratulate each other. Everyone worked together for a cause.

"My brother passed in 1998. He had been an assistant stage manager. He met Annie Taggert at WBT, and they got married. Steve Calleran is the brother-in-law! As I said, I was the stage manager, and my brother was an assistant. On stage was *Best Little Whorehouse in Texas.* It was at the old theatre—I was out in front of the house, taking notes of the performance. I was watching the scene and I didn't understand what was happen-ing. The actors were ad-libbing dialog! My brother and I were watching, perplexed! But—it was my fault! I missed my cue . . . they were waiting for me!

"Ah, memories. *Camelot* was playing in the old building. It was four in morning. I got a call from the police, from the hospital. On a prop table was candy, shellacked and varnished. Unfortunately, a group of Girls Scouts sampled that candy and ended up in the hospital.

"Another fun memory. It was *Annie Get Your Gun.* We had a three-piece combo: a bass, a baby grand, and drums. The musicians sat in the pit, right next to the stage. They were so close, they could touch the stage. The Indians in a coach car scene were acting, naturally. Suddenly, one Indian would peel a banana and throw the peel backstage. Not this time! He through it, and it landed on the drummer's head, like a hat. Frank Nace was the drummer. Everybody thought it was hilarious!

"In WBT, part of my job was to make sure everything went well. Lisa was the production person, the main contact. I was there for tech stuff for every show from 1991 to September 2005. I am always interesting in returning there, but I am really done with theatre. I am a professional photographer now.

"The whole experience working with Bill and Bob was happy."

Thank you, David. As I mentioned, the whole apparatus at An Evening Dinner Theatre/Westchester Broadway Theatre was and is a family experience and a happy one for many people: the people who work there and the audience members!

"It's more than you, it is more than me. No matter what we are, we are a family. This dream is for all of us, this one can be real. *Dreamgirls:* Henry Krieger and Tom Eyen

SCENE TWO:
I CAN DO THAT!

It's time to get a better, larger, more intricate theatre for the producers. It's 1991, times have been good—great—with audiences enthralled (many, many people) with the Evening Dinner Theatre. It was time to move to the Westchester Broadway Theatre—but it hadn't been built yet! The lease on the old theatre was up. These producers were looking around for a new space because of all the new technical things. Things that couldn't be done in the old space. The producers looked around and spoke to other developers. Meanwhile, An Evening Dinner Theatre was constantly sold out, because they had terrific business.

The producers went to Robert Martin/Weinberg in 1991 to find a bigger space. The administrative offices were across the street from An Evening. They needed a central place. The key was, because as the theatre grew, and made excellent money, that they ended up with no clout. Finally they came back to the developers with a proposition to build Westchester Broadway Theatre on an empty lot, with plenty of parking. They took over the idea and agreed to build the building.

They had the talented Judith Chafee to design a new building—with luxury boxes. The architects and others came in. It was said that they were pissed off because she solved all the problems.

An Evening Dinner Theatre had served its purpose. Eighty-three shows had been presented. But when people had to exit for the bathrooms, they went through the dressing rooms. There was no room backstage for scenery, props, costumes. They needed bigger casts for bigger productions. Waiters had to sit in the lobby when they were off; so did some actors. They tried to extend the space for offices—producers, assistant producers, accountants, box office. They had rented space across the street. It wasn't enough. Besides, new hydraulics had come into being. Eventually for the show *Phantom of the Opera,* they would need these hydraulics . . . a bigger stage . . . scenery that didn't have to be carried in . . . bigger fly space for scenery . . . everything!

The producers went to the Candlelight Theatre in Chicago where a guy named Polinsky and a partner put great mechanics into the stage. "We saw *Phantom* there . . . decided we got to do this. Brought them in to fix our new stage." Bill and Bob are talking about the immensely better version of *Phantom of the Opera*, called *Phantom,* by Arthur Kopit and Maury Yeston.

So, the producers had to build a new theatre. You see, their lease was up at An Evening, and, as I said, new things were happening in theatre they couldn't do in the old space. It was new technology. They had looked around and found other places with at least three different developers, but Martin/Weinberg told them he would build for them a beacon for the county. Broadway was changing. Stutler and Funking had to keep up with all changes—that's why they moved. Bankers would not give money!

It was said that they paid for the 'fucking' building at least five times—maybe more! They wanted those special celebrity boxes, too.

They dedicated the building to Richard Casper by putting up a bronze plaque in the lobby.

It reads:

THE RICHARD CASPER LOBBY

RICHARD CASPER
January 21, 1949–August 3, 1990

> *In the lobby of the Westchester Broadway Theatre is a bronze plaque dedicating the lobby to the memory of Richard Casper, an actor, director, and choreographer whose extraordinary talents touched over one third of our productions.*

Richard was with us on our opening night back on July 9, 1974, as a member of the cast of KISS ME KATE. And on that night, we began a collaboration that spanned all 16 years of our history.

At An Evening Dinner Theatre, Richard directed an unprecedented 21 productions. His gift as director/choreographer helped to create some of our biggest successes that provided theatrical delight for hundreds of thousands of our guests. In addition, he performed in six of our shows.

A graduate of Northwestern University, his career as an actor and dancer began with an appearance in the National Company of BUBBLING BROWN SUGAR with Cab Calloway, and was followed by the Broadway production of the New York Shakespeare festival's MUCH ADO ABOUT NOTHING.

Memorable productions that he directed away from An Evening included CABARET with Russ Tamblyn; PETER PAN with Cathy Rigby; JOSEPH AND THE AMAZING TECHNICOLOR DREAMCOAT with Donna McKechnie; and the National Tour of MY ONE AND ONLY.

In his memory, we at the theatre have established a scholarship in his name at Northwestern University. Through the generosity of Richard's friends and colleagues, we are on our way to raising the $25,000 needed for the scholarship to exist in perpetuity. It is hoped that thru the endowment, students will be able to further their education in theatre at Northwestern.

Richard was special to everyone in the theatrical community, and especially to us at the Westchester Broadway Theatre. His talent, humor, and unique spirit are part of our history. He made a tremendous contribution to our success and was a cherished member of our theatre family.

An opening note from Stutler and Funking on the opening of the Westchester Broadway Theatre: "We are delighted to have you as our guests at our new home, **THE WESTCHES-TER BROADWAY THEATRE**. Our new name reflects what we have become. We are the only permanent professional Equity theatre in the country where Broadway performers, directors, and designers gather to create the best of Broadway entertainment.

"In the last 16 years, it has been our privilege to entertain over two million people from all over the tri-state area. And because of this tremendous support you have given us, we are able to claim the title as **THE LONGEST RUNNING 52 WEEK-A-YEAR PROFESSIONAL THEATRE IN THE HISTORY OF THE STATE OF NEW YORK!**

"We've brought back Broadway's oldest tradition with CELEBRITY BOXES. Guests can now enjoy a wonderful dinner and the best of Broadway from their own private dining and theatre viewing boxes, with reserved parking, coatroom, and private powder room facilities.

"Our grand lobby includes the box office, a meeting room, a souvenir boutique, and enlarged restroom facilities. The gallery above, which stretches the length of the lobby, will serve as an ideal spot for private cocktail parties and receptions..

"Of course, the centerpiece of our new home is the stage. To enable us to bring added "theatrical magic" to every production, we have enlarged it and enhanced its functions which will add to the design aspects of every production.

"As we reflect on the past 16 years, we realize we have much to be thankful for . . . the commitment and dedication of our staff, the enthusiasm and loyalty of our audiences, and the outstanding service and cooperation of our suppliers, all of whom have contributed to make us a cultural mainstay of which we can be proud.

"We couldn't have done it without you."

Let's pause for just a second. We know that this entire enterprise started by Von Ann and Bill Stutler and Bob Funking was for profit, correct? It's not like other regional theatres that are nonprofit—for if you're nonprofit you can solicit for funds from many sources. You can ask for grants to keep your theatre afloat. The Stutlers and Bob Funking did indeed start a business, and they wished to make money from it. That's the nature of business in this country. Ask Donald Trump. But hold on, wait a minute. They simply didn't have to make their business enterprise into a *family*? Did they? Did they have to push and push to bring great musical theatre to Westchester? Couldn't they have just settled for second-rate talent? Couldn't they have treated their staff in an aloof, cavalier manner? Couldn't they have just served hamburgers for their meals? Why bother finding the best talent, the best staff, the best chefs, the best associates, the best space, the best accommodations? That simply isn't the way business is conducted. Again, ask Donald Trump. It's cutthroat. It's employer-versus-employer. It's "I don't care—I just want to make money!" Isn't it, ladies and gentlemen of the audience? Don't we all just want to be rich?

It's rare in any business to find such people as Stutler and Funking. It's rare. For you see, they *care*! And they've shown that care over the past forty-three years. Ask their past employees . . . staff . . . actors. Ask anyone who has been part of this enterprise. They never sacrificed quality for the mighty dollar. They never sacrificed excellence for a lucre.

They never sacrificed their theatres for pursuit of the American dream—success. It came to them because they were deserving, and because they *cared*! They cared about the people who worked for them. They cared about quality. They cared about their shows. And they cared about us, the public. Isn't that unique in American business? Isn't that unique in American theatre?

You and I both know it is.

The year is 1991. What was happening in the world? The country? We remember that after Iraq invaded Kuwait, a United Nations Coalition Force led by the United States forced Iraq, and thus we won that war. Freddie Mercury died of AIDS.

The yearly inflation rate was only 4.25 percent, and a gallon of gas cost $1.12. The Dow reached 3169—over 3000 for the first time! Inflation ran rampant. The START treaty started with the Soviet Union in July of 1991. The USSR broke up.

Apartheid ended in South Africa. The Internet reached over one million subscribers. We could see *Silence of the Lambs* in the movies, as well as *Beauty and the Beast*. Bryan Adams sang, "Everything I Do, I Do for You." And, as I said, inflation was rampant in our country.

A perfect time to open a new dinner theatre in Elmsford, dontcha think?

And what better show to open the new Westchester Broadway Theatre, than *A Chorus Line*. February 1991.

Listen to this pedigree: Rob Ashford was the dance captain. Rob Marshall was the director/choreographer, and his sister, Kathleen Marshall, as the assistant director/choreographer. The date: February 1991. The show ran until June. The producers wished it to be two acts in Elmsford . . . but the powers that be commanded that it be done as originally staged on Broadway, in one act. Neither Bob nor Bill liked the representative from the Broadway *A Chorus Line.*

Let's journey back to that show. It's a cold February. Every February is cold. Rob Marshall, director/choreographer's credits in the WBT *Playbill* credited him for a lot of regional theatre work—at Goodspeed Opera House and at the North Shore Music Theatre. He was assistant choreographer on the original Broadway *The Mystery of Edwin Drood.* Remember, please, the year is 1991. Since that time, Mr. Marshall has been part of the following as a director and/or choreographer: *Cabaret* revival; *Seussical; Little Me, A Funny Thing Happened on the Way to the Forum; Victor/Viktoria; She Loves Me; Company.* Mr. Marshall also directed the 2004 best picture, *Chicago*, and won best director. Amazing career for Rob Marshall, who was a "nobody" at Westchester Broadway Theatre in 1991! Amazing!

Kathleen Marshall, his sister, was the assistant director and assistant choreographer at the 1991 Westchester Broadway Theatre *A Chorus Line.* Her credits in 1991 showed that she toured in the national company of *Cats. S*he appeared at An Evening Dinner Theatre in *Drood* and *On Your Toes.* Since 1991, Ms. Marshall has won two Tony Awards for choreography; in 2003 for the revival of *Wonderful Town,* and in 2006 for the revival

of *Pajama Game. S*he directed and choreographed the following on Broadway: *Anything Goes; Nice Work If You Can Get It,* among others, and, in 2016, *In Transit. S*he was, like her brother in 1991 in Elmsford, a "nobody." She became a "somebody" in later years. Like her brother, she got her start with Bill Stutler and Bob Funking.

Rob Ashford. Let's discuss Mr. Ashford. He, as I stated, was the dance captain for the first show at the Westchester Broadway Theatre. Since that time, Mr. Ashford has won a Tony for choreography in 2002 for *Thoroughly Modern Millie;* A Drama Desk Award as well as an Outer Critics Award; an Olivier Award in London for *Anna Christie* direction; and an Emmy for choreography on the 81st Annual Tony Awards Show.

Remember, folks, how the Stutlers and Bob Funking started this "little" theatre in Elmsford. The Marshalls and Mr. Ashford are but a few of the many who trained at their "littler" theatre and rose to great success!

I should mention John Mulcahy, who was the musical director/conductor for WBT's *A Chorus Line. A*gain, at the time, he was busy as musical director and associate artistic director at The Maine State Music Theatre. Today Mr. Mulcahy has been associated with the revival of *Man Of La Mancha* on Broadway, and as the musical director of the revival of *Annie Get Your Gun.*

Amazing, isn't it? And you thought that one small business enterprise—a theatre with dinner—would only generate "small" news. You are wrong. The careers that were born in Elmsford have bloomed on Broadway, London, and Hollywood for audiences of untold numbers.

"Kiss today goodbye, the sweetness and the sorrow. We did what we had to do, and I can't regret What I Did For Love, What I Did For Love: *A Chorus Line*: **Marvin Hamlisch, Edward Kleban**

Westchester Broadway Theatre was a success. Let's plan, now in 1991, for the future:

SCENE THREE:
PEOPLE WHO NEED PEOPLE

In a musical, you have many scenes to illustrate and move the plot forward. The songs are supposed to also advance the plot. (This idea came from the first production of *Oklahoma*.) So, for this musical about how Von Ann and Bill Stutler and Bob Funking created a beacon of musical theatre in Elmsford, New York, with their An Evening Dinner Theatre and then, Westchester Broadway Theatre, we set this scene in this "musical" that will highlight people who need people—and, in Elmsford, "are the luckiest people in the world."

I mentioned a noted producer today on Broadway. His name is Jack Batman. Jack W. Batman, according to his credits, is a Tony Award-winning producer of the following Broadway shows: *Natasha; Pierre and The Great Comet of 1812; On the Town; You Can't Take it With You; I am Harvey Milk; The Scottsboro Boys; Pippin; Clybourne Park; Nice Work if You Can Get It; Bonnie and Clyde; Enchanted April; Carrie, the Musical; By Jeeves; Straight; The 39 Steps; The Judy Show; My Trip Down the Pink Carpet,* and *Clean Alternatives.* His production company is SunnySpot Productions, Inc., at 1650 Broadway, Suite 1407, New York, NY 10019, *sunnyspotproductions.com*

"I first met Bob Funking and Bill Stutler in 1974. I had recently opened a theatre casting business in Manhattan (rare for the time), and my offices were on one floor of a building on West Forty-Eighth Street. The floor above mine was the office of a theatrical design company run by my soon-to-be very good friend Michael Hotopp and his design partner, Paul de Pass. At the time, they had just begun designing the very first show produced at An Evening Dinner Theatre *Kiss Me, Kate.* My services were directed toward out-of-town theatres, both as casting director and as in-town representative, and Michael thought we were a perfect match, so he introduced me to Bob and Bill (and Von Ann). It turns out that he was totally right.

"Almost immediately they engaged me, and the first show that I cast for them was their second offering, *Barefoot in the Park.* I subsequently cast about a dozen different productions for them, right up through the summer of 1976 (and *South Pacific,* I believe), when I bowed out with their blessing to open a theatre in Illinois.

"Working for Bob and Bill was always a real pleasure. We had so much fun in auditions, and we were all delighted with some of the extraordinary actors who came in to see us and were subsequently cast. (I distinctly remember a young Holland Taylor stealing the show as Ruth in Noël Coward's *Blithe Spirit,* and the opening night of *Oklahoma!* when I shared my table with a still-lovely Joan Roberts, who had created the leading role of Laurey on Broadway in 1943.)

"Their beautiful theatre, so close to Broadway, and the quality productions they presented were remarkable at the time and, as a result, wonderful Broadway performers, directors, designers, musical directors, and other fantastically creative people came and conquered. There were many other dinner theatres that popped up after An Evening Dinner Theatre, but it was definitely the "Cream of the Crop, Top of the Heap," and I am so proud to have played a small part in its initial success.

"Through the years we never lost touch, and I have seen many productions both at An Evening and subsequently at Westchester Broadway Theatre. It's really amazing to me that they are still producing at such a remarkably high level and that their audiences are clamoring for more. I thank Bob and Bill and Von Ann every day for believing in me, and I give them a standing ovation for their courage, stamina, good taste, and extraordinary producing skills."

And Jane Bergere, another Broadway producer today: She was the producer at the Darien Dinner Theatre. Bill and Bob swapped people with her periodically. I know this sounds like slavery, but it wasn't.

"I became the producer at the Darien Dinner Theatre. Both Bob and Bill were aware of that fact. We became very good friends; we would go to each others' opening nights. We even shared stage managers! Anything! I once called and told them I needed a stage manager (I had to fire the one I had). I remember that problem very well! For a while I had to fill in as stage manager, but I didn't want to continue doing that—it wasn't my thing. I was in a tough spot. I called them to tell them of my need. Immediately they gave me the number of someone who I hired—luckily! They didn't think twice about it!

"Our paths crossed many times, because we were both trying to do the same thing for our patrons—a dinner theatre. A restaurant and theatre are the best/worst and most difficult businesses. I produced over fifty shows.

"I met them because my husband and I used to go to An Evening Dinner Theatre.

"We went to see their wonderful shows with wonderful quality. They treat people with such respect that people kept coming back, staff, actors, musicians, everybody! They were like that with everybody. As a matter of fact, they became a role model for me. I stole a lot of what they did. It was well worth it. We shared many experiences and shared people. We were very supportive of each other. We became socially very good friends. My late husband and I always went there.

"I've almost become part of the family since then. I spent a lot of time with Bob at his home in Saratoga. Bob is very interested in horses.

"In the nineteen nineties, the Darien owners decided to close the theatre down. I no longer had a job. Even after that, Bill and Bob continuously invited us to their shows. They treat everybody so beautifully. They do an excellent job. They could teach a course! I see people who worked for me at Darien . . . they have not forgotten being there. I got that from Bob and Bill. I saw the way they treated their people . . . Everyone speaks of them very highly. I have never heard anybody say something negative about them. They have an innate ability to make everybody feel at home, and they always find a reason to thank people. Their prices are reasonable, good food, free parking. They always discover new marketing techniques and keep their quality of shows and performers excellent.

"Your book is a book that should be published. There are very few Equity American dinner theatres today. At the time when I was at Darien, there were twenty-seven or more. Now it's down to seven.

"At one time, I was an actress. That was another lifetime."

To interrupt Ms. Bergere just for a second . . . this is what she has done in the past couple of years . . . (Jane Bergere Productions) . . . Tony-award winning producer of: *Kinky Boots; The Front Page; the Crucible; It Shoulda Been You; Annie, Clybourne Park, War Horse, Driving Miss Daisy, A Little Night Music, La Cage Aux Folles, Curtains, Glengarry Glen Ross, Caroline, or Change.* And that's just Broadway.

Now she's one of the producers of the upcoming *Hello, Dolly.* And she is very nice, humble, and outgoing.

She is in awe of what the Stutlers and Bob Funking have created. She also loves peach melbas, which are served as dessert for the dinner meals at the Westchester Broadway Theatre. "I will tell you about their peach melba desserts. In each peach melba, there are two delicious cookies. They discovered I love these cookies. When I go to the show, they automatically bring me a plate of these cookies! That's caring!

"It's a wonderful thing—the Westchester Broadway Theatre, that is only for the entertainment in a community that is deserving of it. It fills a void. They have created a family in which so many people who met there married while working with them. Today even the children and grandchildren of staff workers are working there!

"As for me, I got to Broadway from Connecticut. I was then offered a show that nobody else wanted to do after 9/11. It was called *Metamorphosis.* I was very lucky to get that show. That began my producing career on Broadway. Then I produced *Caroline, or Change.* Someone had asked me, why don't you do musicals? I did so many at Darien. I started then to do them.

"To be a producer means you have to have good taste and love theatre, and you must be able to combine the business part with the aesthetic. It's really named "show business" for a reason! I was told years ago that I should really be a producer, because I have an innate sense of good taste in theatre. I said, this is something I can try in my life . . . I can always go back to acting . . . real estate . . . there are other things I can figure out to do in my life!

"This is very enriching and enticing, and I love the entire aspect of producing, the creativity, the business end of it. I guess I was bitten by the bug!

"You have to want to devote yourself to be creative. Bill and Bob and myself have to have audiences who pay for tickets in order to pay actors, staff, etc. If we were nonprofit theatre, you have to search for shows and ideas that not only work financially but work creatively. With a non-for-profit theatre, you have a board of directors who have to raise the money . . . it is their fiduciary responsibility. You can have sponsors, donors, all sorts of fundraising. People even donate props in a non-for-profit. In Elmsford, and even for me, in New York (she is one of the producers of *Hello, Dolly* with Bette Midler) you have to pay the rent . . . there are so many people involved, unions, actors . . . there's rights . . .

"I still go back to Westchester Broadway Theatre. I guess I'm part of their family!"

"It's good, isn't it? Grand, isn't it? Great, isn't it? Swell, isn't it? Fun, isn't it, Now-a-days. *Chicago*: John Kander and Fred Ebb

You're probably wondering why I put that cover at this particular place in this tribute book to An Evening Dinner Theatre/Westchester Broadway Theatre. That's a picture of Steve Calleran—master MC at both of the theatres owned and operated by the Stutlers and by Bob Funking. If you've been

to either or both theatres, you've seen Steve come out at the intermission to tell the audience of each show the upcoming events; to tell them of special shows upcoming; and to tell them to shut off their cell phones and other hazzeri that might interrupt the performance. He is a mainstay here. He has also done commercials and other professional stuff, but . . . his heart and mind and tall body belong here. By the way, it is *his* picture on that *Playbill!*

"I started here in the early 1980s. In January 1975, I moved from Norfolk, Virginia. I worked at a theatre in Virginia Beach. I directed some shows. One day, someone from An Evening Dinner Theatre came up to me. He suggested I look up Bill and Bob. I did. I came to the theatre, walked in the door, and saw a beautiful lady. She was sitting next to the door. Her name is Jean Taggert. She was working there. At that time she was engaged to someone else at time. I was given the job as handyman. I started doing other things, like scenery, running lights. I worked on a show, *Tom Jones.* At that time I was Non-Equity.

"Then I left until the 1980s. I had been working for Don McPherson, who opened a new theatre in Tennessee. Surprise for me, he had hired me to work there. Jeanie had been working for him for years, and so we were both hired. She did me a favor . . . she very gratefully got rid of her fiancé. Three years later we moved to this area, near Elmsford. Today we're thirty-seven years married. I didn't make a lot of money, but I met my wife.

"Recollections I've got by the thousands. Once we had a cat in old building, named Charlie. Longest time didn't know it was a girl. Lived in offices off lobby. She hung out, stayed in offices. Never ever went out on stage or the dining room. During one holiday show, the set was an old New England inn. The set was covered in dust. It was called *A Christmas Inn.*

"For some reason, Charlie decided to wander out during theatre during the day. Nobody was there. She got under dust cover center stage. And stayed there. The show started. After dinner. It was after eight. [The actress] Carol Woods came in— the maid—with luggage. She drops the bags down on a chair. Woo! Charlie just shot out. Cat turned around and looked back at her. People were amazed!

"In the old building, you walked from the lobby to the rest rooms, down a long hall. As you returned from the rest rooms, you came to the lobby—with a big set of heavy curtains. An older guy during matinee came wandering back. He got caught between the curtains and became disoriented. He saw a doorway to the right, which was an archway to the backstage wings. He got back there. He opens door on stage during *Promises.*

"It had a unit set; nothing changed during the show. The two leads are on stage, in an embrace. Everybody laughed. Man just stood there. 'Look, it's Harry!' He was confused. The actors were not sure what to do. 'Were you expecting someone?' he was asked, as the actors stayed in character. Finally someone took him by the arm to his seat.

"You have to look at it this way. Both Bill and Bob came from advertising. They hated it. Bill grew up in Huntington, West Virginia, not far from the Mountaineer Dinner Theater.

That's the town of Hurricane, West Virginia. It is twenty to twenty-five miles from where he grew up. His parents took him to this dinky little theatre. 'This would be great to have in Westchester.' The idea came to him and his wife.

"Eventually he convinced Bob that it was a great thing to do. At that time, 1974, the number-one failing new business was restaurants. Number two was theatre. What a couple of boneheads—two biggest failures. And they had a new concept. They were visionaries. The formula has worked. These guys had wisdom to get people to work with them who knew what they were doing. They didn't know anything about theatre, costumes, etc. . . . For that expertise, they turned to Von Ann!

"We had people here during our heyday period repeating the same roles they had on Broadway. Take John Tracey Egan, who started in children's theatre. Marc Jacoby starred here.

"They deserve incredible credit. When they opened, it was the height of the energy crisis! You've got to give these guys credit taking an idea that didn't work in so many places. But they succeeded.

"One of the things that prompted us to open the Westchester Broadway Theatre was that the last two or three years in Elmsford—late 1980s—the economy was great. They always got the rights to do great shows—a lot are productions right after their Broadway run. For instance, they got *La Cage* immediately after its Broadway run.

(*La Cage* starred P.J. Benjamin, who is now on Broadway in *Wicked.*)

"Today for the Westchester Broadway Theatre there are very few shows available. They stopped closing on Broadway . . . there were longer runs. Now the economy is not doing well. Each show is forty percent larger, forty percent more expensive, but due to their very good, intuitive management, they have managed for the past forty-three years.

"I have nothing but the highest opinion for both of them. They are different men, with different personalities. They are two very different guys with different ideas. It's just like a marriage . . . this partnership . . . incredibly perfect partnership . . .

complement each other. Bill takes care of production. Bob takes care of the financial end.

"The first couple of years they were both there every night . . . made announcements . . . wore the worst tuxedos incredible you can ever imagine. You remember the style at the time. The big, long Olds. These producers wore plaid, sport tuxedos. What were they thinking to welcome an audience?

"Any way we can make your evening better is the style of Westchester Broadway Theatre. This has always been a family place, with an open-door management style. It was much smaller in the beginning . . . a very small place for offices. The cramped offices had everybody there, including accountants and *Playbill*s, in one room. It was hard getting along, with sometimes people shouting at each other.

"We had kids who started as busboys . . . waiters . . . Jeff Lefriere, now our chief accountant, started as busboy. Also Rich Walls, who began as a waiter, is now in accounting. Bob was best man at his wedding. There are the Jumper family—six brothers all worked here together at one point.

"This place has a great advantage over dinner theatres in the country. You find that very good people who work here won't go anywhere else to work, out-of-town. We do seven, eight shows a week. Actors can take day jobs and work around our schedule, for we are flexible.

"I remember the 2005/2006 New Year's Eve gala. Suddenly the sprinkler system went off at midnight. It hit a whole section of people. It hit the balloons in the center section. We had to pay dearly for cleaning bills and vouchers, which we gave to our patrons—all of whom came back. Loyalty.

"Our staff has tempered their goals for a happy, successful work benefit here at Westchester Broadway Theatre. It is family."

Yes, ladies and gentlemen of the audience. As you can see, from many personalities, working for the Stutlers and for Bob Funking is like becoming part of a special family.

I know you are saying, well, it's a business! I know that! But can you name one business that has engendered the loyalty of its staff—its audience? Well? I worked for the New York Board of Education for thirty years in numerous positions, from teacher to administrator; from theatre producer/director to director of various education programs. I have absolutely no loyalty to them at all. And I would venture to guess that most administrators or teachers who were lucky enough, like me, to work in the worst—and I do mean the worst—high schools in the Bronx, New York, would not show the New York City Board of Education—under a new name today—any loyalty whatsoever. What about you, ladies and gentlemen? Did any of you ever work in a job that treated you as a person—as a member of a special family? Huh?

For instance, let's hear from some audience members. Their names: Ron and Meg Tvert. He is a CPA today. "We have been subscribers since the day the theatre opened and have seen every production produced there as well as many of the specials. When the new theatre was being built, I went over during construction to see the layout and choose my table.

"We have always had a table for four, and during the period from inception to now, we have survived four different couples who joined us until they moved. We have seen the changes from the buffet to the served dinner. We watched Ryan Stutler grow up in the theatre, become our waiter and now restaurant manager. Having seen all the productions, we can honestly say that there have only been two shows we didn't like, but we stayed until the end, as all the actors in all the shows work so hard, they deserve our attention."

And Nancy and Joe O'Leary: "For the past twenty-five years, my husband and I have been enthusiastic patrons of the Westchester Broadway Theatre in Elmsford, New York, and for the past ten years we have expanded our theatre experience and pleasure as subscribers. A gift certificate from dear friends for our twenty-fifth wedding anniversary in 1992 introduced us to this wonderful local world of the most popular Broadway musicals, excellent special shows, and fine dining.

"While the main shows are of necessity formatted to accommodate a smaller venue, we feel that their high caliber is truly equal to any stage performance on the Great White Way. The members of the cast of each show are consummate professionals—uniquely talented and obviously passionate about their craft. And, in our opinion, the cuisine that is offered for dinner is on par with multiple-stars-rated restaurants in Manhattan.

"For the O'Leary's attendance at the WBT has become a family affair. For the wedding anniversaries of our three daughters and sons-in-law, we present them with gift certificates—and they all tell us that we couldn't select a more meaningful and treasured gift to them! We take advantage of the "Christmas in July" promotion, purchasing four gift certificates—three for our children, and keeping one for ourselves! During many Christmas seasons, all of us have celebrated together at the Christmas show on a Friday evening.

"One of the best features of the WBT for us is it's one-stop dining and entertainment experience. As senior citizens in our seventies, we are no longer able to travel into New York City to attend the theatre. It is a pleasure to drive the mere twenty minutes on the Sprain Brook Parkway, from our home in Yonkers to the WBT, and not have to worry about where or how much to park the car.

"The ambiance in the theatre, whatever the time of year, is always festive and mood-enhancing. The host or hostess who greets you and directs you to your seats is so warm and welcoming, you are immediately glad that you decided to spend the evening there. The dinner served, with its vast and varied menu, is invariably scrumptious! The portions are quite generous—we are usually able to take home some of the leftovers for the next day's meal!

"We have long been impressed with the WBT's traditional commitment to and support of developmentally-challenged adults and the agencies which serve them. We look forward participating in the fifty-fifty raffles, the proceeds of which, we have learned, help defray the cost of making the shows available to men and women who could not otherwise afford them, and of surprising special needs children with presents at the Christmas/

Hannukah holidays. We also find the WBT a very convenient drop-off location for our Toys-for-Tots donations.

"As I reminisce on the countless performances at the WBT, which have brought me immeasurable joy, I recall, with great fondness, my attendance at a *Tribute to Elvis* special, about nine or ten years ago. As one of Elvis Presley's most ardent teenybopper fans back in the late fifties and early sixties, I was beyond euphoric when, as the fantastic Elvis impersonator tossed a small, plush teddy bear into the audience (after singing one of his greatest hits, 'Let Me Be Your Teddy Bear,' I reached up and actually caught it in my hands! I do not have the teddy bear anymore (I gave it to my new little granddaughter), but I will always cherish the memory of that precious moment!

"In summary, for my husband and myself in our retirement years, the WBT has become the valued source of so much of our entertainment and dining enjoyment. We look forward to celebrating together our birthdays, anniversaries, and other important occasions at superior musical performances that have always left us feeling uplifted, Inspired, and enriched!"

We go together
Like rama lama lama ka dinga da dinga dong
Remembered forever
As shoo-bop sha wadda wadda yippity boom de boom
Chang chang changitty chang sha-bop
That's the way it should be
—*Grease*: Warren Casey and Jim Jacobs

SCENE FOUR:
COME ON ALONG AND LISTEN TO
THE LULLABY OF BROADWAY

There was a successful run of *A Chorus Line*. It was followed by the following shows, until July of 1992, when the Maury Yeston *Phantom* appeared on stage at the highly thriving Westchester Broadway Theatre: *Gypsy, Annie Get Your Gun,* and *Sugar.*

Phantom, by Maury Yeston and Arthur Kopit, was an interesting show. In January 1991, Houston Texas's Theater Under the Stars presented the world premiere of the Maury Yeston / Arthur Kopit musical, *Phantom*. This was because there was an inferior production by Andrew Lloyd Webber on Broadway. The show then went to Seattle and the California Theatre of Performing Arts and to the Candlelight Playhouse in Chicago. It was raved! The producers were so successful with this *Phantom* that they added *Nunsense* to the bill—at the same time! That had just been released, and luckily, they got it! *Nunsense* ran Monday and Tuesdays and *Phantom* ran the rest of the time.

So, Mr. Robert Cuccioli starred July 1992–April 1993 (Whew! So many successful months!) at the Westchester Broadway Theatre. It was revived in September 1996 and again in December 2007. As I stated, Bob and Bill (the producers) saw it and wanted it for Elmsford. And so it was so!

The original nine-month run brought over 120,000 people to WBT, the longest-running show ever in Elmsford. The show *Nunsense* ran concurrently on nights when the main show wasn't showing.

Following, Susie McMonagle starred as Annie Oakley. She also appeared on Broadway in *Chicago Med*. Peter Reardon played Frank Butler in *Annie Get Your Gun.* You probably

116

remember him from the following Broadway shows: *Irving Berlin's White Christmas; Urinetown; Passion; Meet Me in St. Louis;* and *La Cage Aux Folles.*

It is October 1991. As Bill said, he fired an actress because "her husband was directing a show Off Broadway; she took off without telling anyone . . . she went down there to see her husband's show . . . I fired her. But I lost to Equity."

Moving on with our spectacular view of the American Musical Theatre, as presented by the Westchester Broadway Theatre: I could list all the shows that Stutler and Funking produced in the last eight years of the twentieth century, but I think it's just gilding the canary . . . so . . .

Have you seen any of the following shows on Broadway? Well, they all filled important, successful slots in the 1992–2000 calendar of Westchester Broadway Theatre:

Joseph and the Amazing Technicolor Dreamcoat; Singin' in the Rain; Fiddler on the Roof; Man of La Mancha; West Side Story; La Cage Aux Folles; Funny Girl; My Fair Lady; Grease. Which brings us to Y2K: the year 2000.

Broadway in Elmsford. Didja see Tom Urich in *La Cage*? He reprised his role after appearing in the Broadway production. Didja see Meg Bussert and Mark Jacoby (longest run as the Broadway *Phantom*) in *Chicago*? You know that Meg Bussert appeared as the star in the revivals of *Damn Yankees, Brigadoon,* and *The Music Man.* Also, Ms. Bussert was Judy Kaye's understudy in the original show, *Souvenir,* about Florence Foster Jenkins, who is now being portrayed by Oscar-winner Meryl Streep in the movie of the same name.

Sugar was sweet in 1992. *Grand Hotel* opened in 1993. *City of Angels* landed with Robert Cuccioli in September 1993. Then came *Evita. Sayonara* said hello in May of 1994. But . . . even though it took the same route as *Phantom* (Houston to Chicago's Candlelight) and the producers wanted so much to bring it to Elmsford, "It wasn't as successful because people were mad this year at the Japanese because they were buying everything in the country. Unfortunately, people took it out on WBT! They didn't come to see the show!"

117

Brigadoon followed. Now we're in 1994. *Pirates of Penzance,* then *Gigi,* in May of 1994. "It's so funny how many times Glory Crampton and Robert Cuccioli were paired! Of course, they're married to others . . ."

Dreamgirls in 1995 had Julia Lema as Effie White. Ms. Lema appeared in *Pal Joey* with Lena Horne and Clinton Davis; *Leader of the Pack; Ain't Misbehavin'; Honky Tonk Nights* and *Guys and Dolls* on Broadway. Brian Evaret Chandler, who played Curtis Taylor, Jr., appeared in Broadway's *Timon of Athens.*

In 1996, at Truman High School in the Bronx, I was the theatre administrator/producer/director. The populace of the school had changed over the past twenty years, and now most of the students were minority. I thought *Dreamgirls* would be an excellent show to perform for the student population and their parents and for the community of Co-Op City, where the school was situated.

The previous summer, I had the privilege of teaching summer school in New York City, at Washington Irving High School—at night. Some of you might remember—that was the summer when a week in late July the temperatures were over a a hundred degrees for a couple of days. Well, the school had no air-conditioning, and each class was one and a half hours long.

One girl approached me during one of my l-o-o-ong classes and introduced herself to me. Her name was Princess. She knew I was in charge of theatre at Truman High School. She told me that she would be transferring there in September. She was interested in being in a show—she was an actress. She passed my class.

To make a short story long, she was chosen as Effie in the Truman High School spring production of *Dreamgirls.* We built a long platform, out into the audience, just for her solo of "I'm Telling You I'm Not Going." She brought down the house. I truly believed this girl would make it professionally.

But it was not to be. Her former boyfriend, with whom she had a child, shot her in a parked car in the area known as the Valley—crime-ridden Valley. She was with her current boy-friend. She died. She was eighteen years old.

118

Why I am relating this story? Because the story of Westchester Broadway Theatre is not only the story of Westchester Broadway Theatre, it is the story of life. Theatre mirrors life; life mirrors theatre. And when we see a musical play, such as the many exceptional ones produced by Funking and Stutler, it awakens memories in ourselves—we see our lives. And that is the beauty of theatre—and the beauty of the Westchester Broadway Theatre.

Guys and Dolls returned to the Westchester Broadway Theatre in September 1995. *Joseph and the Amazing Technicolor Dreamcoat* graced the stage next. *Singing in the Rain* followed.

You remember, of course, New Year's Eve (as recounted by Steve Callerhan, that during the show it actually rained on the audience. As Susan Carlson remembers, "We were sitting in the one-hundred row for *Singing in the Rain*, and we were getting very wet as the rain fell from a pipe above the stage!"

The story about the late Peter Allen, *The Boy from Oz,* followed. Then *Phantom* returned. *The King and I* came to Elmsford, starring Martin Vidnovic. "This brilliant actor had to have a phone in his office to talk to someone each day to prop him up. He was terrific; unfortunately, he quit during the run of the show. David Edwards took over." As you know, Martin Vignovic's credits include *Footloose; King David; Guys and Dolls; Brigadoon; Baby.* His daughter is Laura Benanti, who won a Tony last year for *She Loves Me.* That's also to his credit.

Ah, the history of American musical theatre, through the journals of two ex-accountants who formed a theatre in Westchester. Wouldn't this make a great movie? Huh, wouldn't it?

Moving on with our history. Did you know that the actress Marla Schaffel was a "pain in the ass" and so were the choruses for the show *West Side Story*, in November 1997? Yup. I must interject here, if I might. I was lucky enough to have been a teacher/administrator/theatre director in the worst high schools in the Bronx. I had similar problems with *West Side Story.* I planned to present the show in the spring, so I cast many students for roles. Unfortunately, they fought (literally fought) with each other. The one shining light was a student of mine, a young

119

girl at the time named Charmaine Martinez. She choreographed a dance from the show *America*, and it was as good as anything on Broadway—or at Westchester Broadway Theatre.

Ah, memory lane . . . *La Cage Aux Folles; Funny Girl* (with Jill Abramowitz as Fanny Brice.) It is 1998, and the month is July. Ms. Abramowitz would later understudy Golde in the revival of *Fiddler on the Roof.* She also added lyrics to the song "What They Never Tell You" in *It Shoulda Been You.* She was also in the cast, natch. *C*inderella and *9 to 5* were also shows on Broadway Ms. Abamowitz appeared in.

My Fair Lady came to the theatre in 1999, with Kim Lindsay. (*Titanic, Show Boat,* and *Les Mis* on Broadway . . . her credits.)

You can notice a pattern. WBT got the best shows to Elmsford—sometimes directly from Broadway. And its cast members, all union, eventually went to greater fame on Broadway. Imagine a room in 2017, filled with former cast members of the Stutler/Funking shows. There would be more stars there than in heaven! (I stole this quote—sorry.)

The producers visited *Oklahoma* and *Camelot* in 1999. They also visited *42nd Street.* In 2000 (after Y2K), *The King and I* returned with Stacey Fernandez. "This guy was a big pain in the ass. He wouldn't go on stage barefoot, had to have special sandals. We got rid of him and brought in someone else." That's show biz, folks.

Let's continue our tour down WBT memory lane: *Grease; The Sound of Music; Crazy for You* in October of the millennial year. Melissa Hart played Dolly Levi in the WBT production of *Hello, Dolly* in February of 2001. Kurt Peterson played the Bing Crosby part in *High Society.*

It would have been *A Wonderful Life*—without the word "It's" because the producers were prohibited for the Christmas season of 2001 from using the full title. That, also, is show biz!

Let's take a break from my narrative . . . I'd need three books to list all the people who were actors in Elmsford, New York! Thank you, Von Ann Stutler, Bill Stutler, and Bob Funking, for your family—a theatrical family—that you created!

Didja know that dignitaries for China, Britain, France, and Russia came to WBT? Didja know that children's shows were held on Saturdays in the summer and there were specially priced Wednesday nights . . . didja know that each holiday season, children from many institutions have been invited, free, to see the musical productions? Each institution receives money for gifts from the fifty/fifty raffle each holiday season. Didja know that Funking and Stutler donate—yes, this "business" donates—gifts, such as televisions, stereos, computers, to these institutions?

Didja know that the following charities are recipients of money from Westchester Broadway Theatre? They are: God's Love We Deliver; Equity Fights Aids; American Cancer Society; American Heart Association; Westchester Gilda's Club.

That's a pretty impressive resume for the family at the Westchester Broadway Theatre. Let's ask an actor how it was to work for this unique theatre.

Victoria Fraser worked at An Evening Dinner Theatre. She worked there with enthusiasm. She walked into an audition with her picture and resume. She was Non-Equity, didn't belong to the union, at the time. "The first person I see is a handsome guy in a suit—that was Bill. He spoke to me for a while. I told him that I wanted to audition. He was so busy and so kind. We chatted and chatted away, and I ended up in the ticket office for one year.

"Little by little, to make a long story short, I eventually got my Equity card with the show *Play It Again, Sam.* I got another job in an Equity show . . . the bottom was that I knew the director Roseanne Weeks. I played three characters in it. The best thing for me was that I had a great time. There was one exit one night. I fell off an exit ramp and broke a foot. I played the rest of show with a cast. I ended up in Jack O'Brian's column in the *New York Post.* I was told to 'break a leg,' so I did.

"At An Eve, you had to go out to the buffet. The actors could partake whenever they wanted. There I am, not working at the time, standing in line for roast beef. Behind the chef on the wall there is this big picture of Vanessa—the character I played, in my red wig and leopard dress. Talk about that show biz, baby! I was there, waiting in line for roast beef, looking at my glory days.

"There isn't a show now on Broadway that doesn't have an alumnus from An Evening or Westchester Broadway Theatre. I remember Estelle Harris. I remember Marsha King—crazy as a loon. There was never a star like Estelle. This was a funny start for her, for her career. Boy, those people worked hard in Elmsford—I don't know how they did it. They put everything into it. I'm sorry that after appearing there I went out on the road, and never got back . . . you just move on . . .

"I am now retired for three years. I do voice-overs, commercials. If ever an opportunity came to come back, I would. I got my start there! I had a wonderful time with them. They were just wonderful people to work with; they made it like a family."

And Marylin Gabriel . . . in the costuming department: "I took a not-so-graceful flying flop upon entering the waiters' room. The waitstaff was very busy napkining, rolling, basketing, etc. All eyes followed my descent to the floor. All hands continued their assigned tasks. Not a word was spoken, but I was laughing hysterically! I'm sure that everyone else did, too! After I left!

"I learned the computer!!!!!

"I made an emergency zipper repair for Michael Osteen on his yellow dress for *Sugar* in about three minutes. I almost had to go on stage with him!

"I used to be known as the "coffin lady," for the coffins I had to dress for *Big River* and *Evita*.

"I caught a customer in my arms as she tripped over the curb right outside the building!

"I arranged for a first wedding cake for a couple's fiftieth anniversary—they had never had a wedding cake because they were married on the road tour of the original *Showboat*!"

What about hearing from an agent? B. Lynne Jebens: "I started as an agent in 1980. There were so many wonderful regional theaters around in those days, but the dinner theatres had already started to fade. Westchester Broadway Theatre is one of the last of a genre that holds a fond place in my heart.

There were a number of them in the Chicago area when I was growing up, and they were a delight to attend.

"As I started booking actors at the American Arts, Film and Television Academy, the treat was to be able to go up and see my actors perform. I have always been impressed with the level of professionalism that Westchester Broadway Theatre has been able to maintain. It was obvious that the men running the theatre cared about the quality of the work that was being done there. The best way of telling that is that the actors want to return and work there again and again. Just like a family. I have the deepest respect for this theatre."

"I could have danced all night! I could have danced all night! And still have begged for more. *My Fair Lady*: Alan Jay Lerner and Frederick Loewe

Stories! I got lots of stories! So many stories. Take Mr. Don DeCarlo. "I began performing at An Evening Dinner Theatre in special Monday night shows at the age of eighteen, back in 1978. When they designed the Westchester Broadway Theatre, I continued with special shows, publicity junkets, and children's theatre, both onstage and backstage. I worked closely with George Puello, one of their artistic directors, both on and off-stage for years and have loved every minute of it.

"Life being what it is, I now have an internet show on Blog Talk Radio called 'Word of Mom Radio,' so for the past few years I'm one of the press that is invited to opening night galas. It is exciting to share the WBT and the fantastic performers they continually cast on my show. We celebrated their fortieth anniversary with 'The Women of WBT,' led by Von Ann Stutler herself!

"It has been an honor and a privilege to know Bob Funking and Bill and Von Ann Stutler for most of my life, and I'm happy to say my children know them too! What marvelous traditions they have created, giving countless families the gift of Broadway theatre right in our own backyard!"

And now a word from a famous reviewer! Patti Chattman. "Yes, I am Gary's wife but still think I deserve the chance to tell you how wonderful WBT is! I've been coming here even when there was an Evening Dinner Theatre, over forty years ago.

"We've been coming here faithfully as regular people until recently, when Gary Chattman, my husband, became a writer, but I am not. I am a faithful theatregoer. I am from Manhattan, and I love Broadway. Your productions are so consummately professional,*and the locale is so convenient, and your staff is amazing. My daughter was born in April 1973, and soon thereafter, 1974, your regional site theater in Elmsford opened. We were long-standing fans since you opened. We have come here to share joyful times, now precious memories with parents who have passed. We brought our children when they were young enough to be not ashamed to be with their parents!

"Now a new generation continues for us. It's bringing joy to attend many shows with our eleven-year-old grandson, Ryan. It is a precious time to share with him alone – he's been mesmerized by theater productions here! His first *Fiddler on the Roof!* Anniversaries come in time, including ours; birthdays of all living family and our deceased relatives. We are but a few miles from WBT, and your shows have always brought smiles to the faces of those who came with us—and to us as well. These are faces of joy, frozen in time for us because of you.

"Thank you for all the memories. Thank you for being a tradition. Our family thanks you for your professional productions and superior cuisine. I cherish you and your owners and staff. We look forward to your June production of *Annie,* so we can introduce our five-year-old grandson, Noah, and our two-year-old grandson, Zachary, to your wonderful theatre."

Time marches on. But WBT continues on, and we revel in its endurance and ability to entertain audiences with the very best in musical theatre.

"You're a special kind of people known as show people; You live in a world of your own. The audience paid plenty to sit there and clap; hearing you sing, watching you tap." *Curtains*: **John Kander and Fred Ebb**

SCENE FIVE:
MAMMA MIA, HERE I GO AGAIN

You're probably thinking that the song is apropos—from *Mamma Mia,* which will be the next star production at Westchester Broadway Theatre in March of 2017. You're right. Funking and Stutler just keep cranking them out!

For instance, my wife and I saw a show last night there titled *The Bikinis.* It's fashioned as a feminine answer to *Jersey Boys.* You are probably asking, huh? *The Bikinis*! Well, let me tell you what a fabulous show it was. Here, read my review, taken from the very-famous *Westchester Arts and Education Review,* of which I am publisher: GARY CHATTMAN,

PUBLISHER/CRITIC
THE BIKINIS
WESTCHESTER BROADWAY THEATRE
THROUGH MARCH 19, 2017

125

There is a cast appearing in a show at the spectacular Westchester Broadway Theatre in a production called THE BIKINIS. Now, don't be thrown off by the title. It's a story of four girls who turned into ladies who formed a group (like the "Jersey Boys") and appeared at a trailer park in New Jersey and then eventually found fame by creating their very own '45 record! Remember those!

Katy Blake, Anne Fraser Thomas, Joanna Young and Karyn Quakenbush play the girls. Just sit back and enjoy a bunch of '60s music, sung as professionally and powerfully as you can imagine. Just sit back and enjoy your dinner; don't worry about your car (free parking) and tilt those swivel chairs to the best angle to make you comfy. Each and every one of these ladies is terrific, but I'm gonna single out two: Katy Blake (writing her own musical now; starring at the Pasadena Playhouse; starring in Andrew Lloyd Webber's "Whistle Down the Wind," "Evita," "The Phantom of the Opera." And there's Karyn Quakenbush (understudy for Bernadette Peters and Reba McEntire in "Annie Get Your Gun" and has appeared as Diana and Val in "A Chorus Line." Boy, these ladies can SING!

I'm not taking anything away from Anne Fraser Thomas ("Man of La Mancha," "How the Grinch Stole Christmas") and Joanna Young ("Drowsy Chaperone" and "Grease!') for, as a group, this GROUP can entertain!

The audience went "wowsa" after each rollicking song. Let's see, you've no doubt heard these songs (even if you are too young to have experienced them) many times: You might have heard them "Under the Boardwalk," or in a "Chapel of Love;" You might have gone "Where the Boys Are" or in a "Heat Wave." You might remember "Walking in the Sand." No doubt you wondered, as a teenager, "When Will I Be Loved," but today, you're sure that any "Simple Song of Freedom" can be "Dedicated to the One I Love." Us oldsters remember that "Itsy Bitsy, Teeny Weeny, Yellow Polka Dot Bikini" and "The Twist." We even might have, as teenagers, indulged in "Incense and Peppermints." But you, my Westchester audience, don't have to wonder, this January, at this "Time of the Season," about a "Mambo Italiano" or "Hava Nagila." No, you make sure you go to the Westchester Broadway Theatre and see THE BIKINIS. Because it's great! It's wonderful! It's nostalgic! The cast is professional (you can't expect anything less from WBT). Remember, "These Boot Are Made for Walkin'"—so walk to Elmsford, or else, maybe a "Secret Agent Man" might not give you that "Simple Song of Freedom."

You've got my drift. Westchester Broadway Theatre, this February. The Cast:

Anne Fraser Thomas, Joanna Young, Karyn Quakenbush, Katy Blake

Alan Gruet was a big part of the success at the Westchester Broadway Theatre. He worked twenty-two years there. "I was an actor in the 1970s, then I started as box office manager. I was always looking for something to do, a professional actor looking to do something. In the original *Fiddler* I played Perchik. I was in the show, Off-Broadway, *The Rothschilds.* Sherman Yellin is my business partner. Wally Harper was my partner for many, many years. I knew him since 1959; we were roommates in college. He was a voice teacher, did arrangements. He was my long-time friend; I travelled with him all over the world. He was the long-time friend and accompanist to Barbara Cook.

"I came to An Evening in 1986. We had dinner. After that, Bill asked me to become box office manager. I told him 'I didn't know how.' He said, 'Didn't know? You'll learn, you'll learn.' I was there six years, ready to leave. It became very difficult. Nobody else had ever lasted that long. Bobby Fitzimmins took over publicity when my theatre connections came into play. We did a benefit for Engine 33, Ladder 51 with Barbara Cook, and raised a hundred thousand dollars for them!

"I was responsible . . . I had connections . . . I started out before we did the *Phantom* by Maury Yeston. I had a connection with Howard Kissel, from the New York *Daily News*. He was a neighbor. I said to him, 'Why don't you come up and see *Phantom*—he wrote a wonderful, glowing review! It ran nine months. We added *Nunsense*. Unfortunately, we had to close when we were selling out. Kissel said, 'The real phantom is at Westchester Broadway Theatre, not on Broadway. I agree. I've seen the real *Phantom* three times.

"I left twenty-two years later. I had started to commute against traffic. I never knew when I would get to the theatre or get home because of the traffic. I would hop on parkways—under construction. I couldn't do it anymore.

"Both Bill and Bob are very clever guys. They used their expertise in advertising to advance the theatre; they were very good at it. They were great with casting. I worked more with Bill.

"I was at auditions. When Robert Cuccioli walked in, I said to Bill, 'That's the guy.' He agreed. Cuccioli had played Nathan in *The Rothschilds*. Then he starred in it—last year, I believe.

"I never would have stayed at the box office. When Bill offered me press director, he took me out to dinner. He told me that 'I'll learn,' when I protested I knew nothing. I learned.

"What I loved about my job was my personal connection with critics. Now it's all changed today, all online. It's not my stuff. I lost the excitement. That's why I retired.

"I was in contact with Jacques Le Sourd, from *The Journal News*. He was a difficult person. Because of my personality, I was able to work with him. I sweet-talked him to write about *Phantom* . . . I used personal relationships for my job, to find people to publicize the theatre for free. I used my access skills for that. I was good at it!

"Nobody retires for one reason . . . there was nothing more for me to learn in the theatre . . . as I said, it's different today. I knew the personal attributes and was familiar with a lot of actors. I knew who to cast. Then they didn't need me.

"Anyway, Wally died, left me all his music. His show: *Josephine Tonight*, about Josephine Baker, ran in the nonprofits, in San Diego, in Chicago. Today 'you can't get arrested here unless you have money.' Yellin/Harper were collaborators. Josephine Baker known in Europe by both Blacks and whites . . . most people who showed up in the theatre were white.

"I have never made any enemies in the theatre, because you never know who you will work with. For instance, there was the feud between Jerry Bock and Sheldon Harnick. I didn't choose sides. They never brought their quarrel into their work.

"If they hadn't moved from An Evening to the new building, they wouldn't have survived. There were many naysayers who said Stutler and Funking got too big too quickly. That's not true. It was the right decision. Technologically, that's where theatre was going. 'Some say that the theatre is dying . . . but it certainly has changed.'"

It's 2017, and the Westchester Broadway Theatre is still presenting quality shows in Elmsford, New York. That dream that two ex-account executives had in the early 1970s has come to fruition, and then some. We will see the Broadway hit *Mamma Mia; Annie* returns in June (for the first time in decades). That great Irving Berlin show *Annie Get Your Gun* follows next fall. No, it isn't a sequel to *Annie!*

You go to Broadway today and you pay unheard-of prices, like $165 or more per show. There are premium seats to the upcoming *Hello, Dolly*, with Bette Midler and David Hyde Pierce, and they are $250-$300!!! I'm sure the show will be great, but who in heaven has that amount of money? You can go today to the Westchester Broadway Theatre and pay a *fraction* of that, and get a great meal and free parking. Need I say more? Have I said more? Will I say more? You betcha!

"Don't tell me not to fly, I've simply got to. If someone takes a spill, it's me and not you. Don't bring around a cloud to rain on my parade." *Funny Girl*: **Bob Merrill and Jule Styne**

SCENE SIX: . . . ARE THE LUCKIEST PEOPLE IN THE WORLD

Letters . . . we get letters . . . How many of you are old enough to remember that phrase from the *Perry Como Show*? Well . . . I guess this dates me . . .

Peter Barierri was the tech director for twenty years as well as a set designer. His first show for WBT was *A Chorus Line*. He was working on Broadway for the show *On Your Toes* as a Broadway technician. "I don't remember how I got the call . . . somebody recommended me. I didn't know where Westchester County/Elmsford was. I simply had no idea. They wanted me to drive up there? Where is this place?

"You can write a whole book about my experiences there. They opened the new theatre. It was terribly exciting. A *Chorus Line* was directed by Rob Marshall. He's a big shot today.

"My highlight was doing changeovers. You see, on Saturday night you take out the old set from the show that was ending. Then you put up a new one. You would find actors on stage Monday night for spacing rehearsal. We had to work over forty-eight hours with round-the-clock crews to fix up to get the new set ready for Monday night. This involved installing hydraulics, tracks, etc. There was the whole scenic/production aspect. You had to take down the old set and fix the automation. You needed slider tracks to move all the scenery. That's the way the system is designed . . . automation, trap doors, turntable.

"The show *Phantom* was when we put the center in. *Phantom* transformed theatre. We put in catwalks. The musicians were moved upstairs. I was working myself to the bone around the clock. We added a top on it—so there could be two levels for *Jekyll and Hyde*.

"Bill and Bob were surrogate fathers when I worked there. We were very close for a very long time. One time, I remember, I injured my hand and couldn't work. Bill was very good to me. Bill said, "You know, I have a house at Candlewood Lake. Come on up. We'll spend the day together. And so, we did. I spent the day on his boat and stayed for a barbecue. What a nice man. He took me under his wing. Working at Westchester Broadway Theatre was such an amazing experience. I could no longer work around-the-clock. I became associate director for Curtain Call in Stamford, Connecticut, and I freelance with design now.

"I left after *The Producers.* At that point I was designing, not doing tech direction, like I did before. I moved to Connecticut and got married and our paths separated. When Bob Durso (a technician) died, I saw everybody at the funeral.

"Westchester Broadway Theatre is more family-oriented, not only for the audience but for the people who work there."

Ladies and gentlemen, do you notice a common thread with the stories of people who worked for the Stutlers and for Bob Funking? Family. They all mention family—and not only for the audience. As I have said, and will say again, this business is unique in this country for the care given to its staff and the feelings engendered by its owners.

And . . . George Dacre, of WRCR and the *Rockland County Times*. He has been reviewing WBT for forty-one years. "What a run! Bob Funking and Bill Stutler are the best!"

And Kevin Borelchard Sr. "I have been coming here from the mid-seventies. Back then, there were meals on a buffet. In the summer of 1979, I took my girlfriend. At the time I took her to see the oldies night. After the show, I asked her to marry me, and she said yes. We come here to two, three times a year, and we have never missed a Christmas show. We have been married thirty-six happy years." Now that's a story!

Ladies and gentlemen, meet Kathleen Conroy, a great storyteller, who for many years was a group sales manager. She remembers . . . "IBMers and the mouse. There were approximately five hundred people entering the theater at six o'clock in the evening, and we spotted a mouse in the stage-left buffet. The staff scrambled to kill it or catch up with it with the drink trays. They got it just in time, and they carried it out on the tray, high over the guests' heads! Can you imagine that?

"I managed the theater on Thanksgiving, and Tony Dinis (the head chef at that time) had decorated the *Pirates of Penzance* ship in the lobby. During intermission, some of the audience members opened the ropes to get to it and were tearing off all the decorations for souvenirs, including the bread cornucopias, which were glued on!

"The first night I house-managed in this building, I locked myself out of the fire escape door. Then, one time, one of the group leaders was sitting in the office making arrangements and gazing dreamily at the statue prop from the *La Cage,* and he said, 'It reminds me of Hawaii.'

"Two very conservative Fortune 500 executives were brought into the group sales office and were sitting next to a large, stuffed *Best Little Whorehouse* doll. For one of them, the situation was just too much, and he moved to a chair with a pillow on it. The pillow is a battery-operated, vibrating model! As he sat there, we were all painfully aware of the fact it was vibrating rather noisily, for some reason. No one said anything, and he betrayed no emotion on his face!

"A dissatisfied customer was yelling in the theater about how unhappy he was with his seats. As I approached him from behind, he said to the other people at his table, 'I'm going to get the manager, make him give us another table. I know how to take care of these guys!' When I introduced myself as the manager, he was so taken aback and became very meek. He told me, 'I just wanted to tell you how much we like it here!' Obviously, this was a few years back.

"Patrick Mcgillicuty came into our office during a rainstorm with a stray dog in tow that he had found outside. I said. 'Oh, what a cute dog' and begin to pet it, but it smelled awful. I asked him to please take it out of the theater, which he did. A few hours later he called me to say that the dog had given birth to a litter of puppies in the backseat of his car on the way to the

Humane Society. When he got there, they made him pay fifteen dollars for each pooch. He then drove home, and his wife Alice wouldn't let him in the house until she hosed him off in the yard because he smelled so bad!

"I was asked to be in on one of the Bobby Fitzsimmons' shows as a last-minute replacement. I had ten minutes of rehearsal and played four parts. With the little time I had, I could only learn my lines and scenes. During the show, Bobby would take me to each entrance to push me on stage when it was time. I pretended to sing the songs. I never knew what the show was about. All I remember is Bob Funking saying, 'It's not dignified for a sales manager to be running around in a banana suit!' PS, it was a corn suit, Bob!"

And that's Westchester Broadway Theatre, folks!

Lisa Bernardin writes, "As a young girl growing up on Long Island, my grandma there would always tell us about a dinner theatre in Westchester that her senior group would frequent. Forty years later, my son performed at WBT for four different shows. Every time I come to the WBT, I remember my grandmother and also seeing my son perform."

Emily Groenendaal relates, "I have so many fond memories from WBT. My family has seen countless shows, all of which were/are excellent. One of my favorite shows is *Nine*, not only because my mother was the musical director, but because the singing was incredible. From the people to the service to the atmosphere, the WBT has always been welcoming and joyous. We also love the peach melba dessert and always think of the family of the WBT when it's mentioned. And Steve is the best MC!"

"I received a Lifetime Achievement Award at this theatre—where one hundred of my friends and relatives attended. I see every show that opens here and always enjoy being here. Where can you get free parking, a class A show, and a delicious meal for such a low cost? The productions are top-drawer, and the technical aspects are equally as good. This is theatre at its best—close to home, and this theatre gives an unknown talent a chance to be seen and recognized!"

The actress who has appeared the most times (sixteen, we figure) at the Westchester Broadway Theatre is Michelle Dawson.

As she says, "I've been lucky enough to work. In 1995, I believe my first show at Westchester Broadway Theatre was *Carousel.* I played Julie Jordan. I had just finished up *Showboat* in New York. It was my first regional lead. Gosh, I've been in so many shows there! At least sixteen! I think *Mamma Mia* next month is the sixteenth! I remember that I replaced Maria . . . I played Mary Magdalene in *Jesus Christ, Superstar* and Lucy in *Jekyll and Hyde.* I did that show twice. I also was Elsa in *Sound of Music;* Nancy in *Oliver;* Glinda in *The Wizard of Oz. I* just finished up as Candy in *Saturday Night Fever.* I've also done a lot of Christmas shows there.

"Actors today are desperate for jobs; we want to keep theatre alive; not as many opportunities. The idea of medical insurance for working is huge for actors!" I interjected that I had been told that many actors keep their day jobs and still act at WBT. She agreed.

"WBT has been around a long time, and everyone knows about it. Actors want to work there because of its reputation. For me, it's a fortunate job because I live in Tappan, New York, and it's the best commute ever for me. I still audition in New York. My husband is a violinist with *The Great Comet.* I teach private students vocal technique, how to warm up, how to interpret a song.

"Once, many years ago, I had a difficult time. Bob and Bill were incredibly supportive. This place is definitely a family, a wonderful place to work. I owe so much to them, and to Lisa Tiso, for helping to keep my career alive. They stretched my abilities beyond what I could do. Out of college, I was an ingénue soprano. I have a pop voice, but they got me started singing in contemporary musical theatre with *Jekyll and Hyde.*

"If they didn't believe in me—especially Lisa Tiso—I wouldn't be who I am. Lisa is a great role model. I feel that once you have negative expectations, they can eat at you. Even though I've worked there many times, they don't just hand things to me. I have to prove myself. Lisa is tough as nails, with the biggest heart ever. Just like family. I can be that insecure actress, and Lisa always says 'get over it' by being the most positive. She believes in me. She props me up.

"At the beginning of each show, Bill comes down to talk to the actors, giving a welcome speech. Bob is more in the background. Lisa is always present.

"For me, especially, they stretched me. For the show *Saturday Night Fever*, I had never sung disco. They believed in me.

"Remember, you have to keep that business, keep it up-to-date. The fact that the Westchester Broadway Theatre is still alive is miraculous!"

Michelle returns to WBT (once again) in March of 2017, playing the part of Donna in *Mamma Mia*. It isn't her first time in the part, however. In July of 2016, she played the part at the John W. Engeman Theater in Northport. The article (in the *Long Islander News*) states that Ms. Dawson was "born and raised in Vermont" and that she wanted to be an actress from a young age. "I got bit by the bug early on and didn't look back!"

The article goes on to state that "at the age of 18, she was crowned Miss Vermont to compete in the Miss America pageant. She has appeared on *Broadway in Cyrano—The Musical; Spider Man—Turn Off the Dark; Showboat* and *Mamma Mia*.

"I toured for over two and a half years with *Mamma Mia*! It was an absolute highlight in my career. I performed "Dancing Queen" on national television at the 2009 Tony Awards."

As I mentioned, she will appear at WBT in March in the same roll. "One of the reasons audiences love it so much is because we are real people. Donna's a mother—she's a single mother—and she has a lost love, and I think a lot of people can relate to that . . . she's earthy and she works hard, you know, running the joint and doing it all on her own and not really taking a moment to think about herself and what she wants."

That quote partially explains the WBT's connection to Michelle Dawson. The difference is that she loves WBT—this family—and she can relate to the Elmsford audiences because, as she said, they are real people—and Michelle Dawson is also a real people, too.

Sherman Yellin, the noted librettist and author, went to the Westchester Broadway Theatre. He went there with Wally Harper, who was Barbara Cook's long-time accompanist. He said, this noted librettist and author, that "All shows of the Westchester Broadway Theatre are professionally done, and superbly cast." He also remembers that once, after a rehearsal, he and his wife drove Barbara Cook home and got lost for four and one half hours looking for the Saw Mill Parkway.

Mr. Yellin is now eighty-five years old and working with Sheldon Harnick on the Off-Broadway show *The Rothschilds*. One thing that he said to me was brilliant, about himself, but I think it could be applied 100 percent to Bill Stutler and Bob Funking. He said that both he and Sheldon Harnick got the "luck of the genetic draw." So did Bob and Bill.

Barbara Cook appeared at WBT in a benefit for the American Red Cross and the World Trade Center Victims Fund, right after 9/11. She remembers it fondly. She was there with her lifetime accompanist, Wally Harper.

Bill and Bob wrote a special thank you:

"We want to take this opportunity to profusely thank all that are present tonight. As soon as we announced this Fund Raiser of the Red Cross Victims Fund, the tickets went flying out the door. We were not surprised because we know that our patrons are very special and will always come through when called upon. We also want to thank all the many patrons who participated in the Westchester Broadway Theatre ticket raffle since September 14th, which alone has raised over $40,000.

A very special thanks goes to all those that are generously donating their services tonight: performers, musicians, stage crew, dining room and kitchen staff, as well as all the other members of our staff that have helped make this night such a tremendous success. And finally, this show could not have taken place without the effort and dedication of Donald Birely, Rick Church, and

*George Puello, who put tonight's show together for all
of you to enjoy.*
   Thank you all, and God Bless America.

Please notice that the entire show was for charity, right after
9/11. Please notice that it is very rare in business—especially
the theatre business—to donate a whole tribute show to causes.
Please notice that Bill Stutler and Bob Funking are unique.

**"When you walk through a storm, hold your head up
high. And don't be afraid of the dark. At the end of
the storm is a golden sky, and the sweet, silver song of
a lark. Walk on, through the wind, walk on through
the rain, tho' your dreams be tossed and blown. Walk
on, walk on, with hope in your heart, and You'll
Never Walk Alone, You'll Never Walk Alone."** *Carousel***: Richard Rodgers and Oscar Hammerstein II**

SCENE SEVEN:
TIME OF THE SEASON

Since this is a theatre, and we are watching a show about the lives of Bill Stutler and Bob Funking, and we're now in ACT II, it would behoove me to change the format a bit. I've chronicled so far, in time, historically, the shows that have appeared on the stages of An Evening Dinner Theatre and Westchester Broadway Theatre. We know that Michelle Dawson starred (her fifteenth WBT show!) in *Saturday Night Fever.* Jacob Tischler (Tony Manero) was in *Flashdance, The 39 Steps, Spamalot,* and *Mary Poppins* at regional theatres. *Miss Saigon* on Broadway had, as one of its stars, Pat McRoberts (Monty in WBT's *Saturday Night Fever.*) Ann-Ngaire Martin, one of the stars of *Christmas Inn,* "went to NYC at eighteen with two hundred and fifty dollars in my pocket and a dream. I lived in a girls' boarding house for a week, till I got a waitressing job. Then I enrolled at the American Academy of Dramatic Arts for a two-year program." She has performed in six WBT shows. She was in Broadway's *Grease* in 1972.

2015: What a year! The producers kept cranking out those wonderful shows! Michelle Dawson (you now know who she is) played Aldonza in *Man of La Mancha.* Paul Schoeffler (from Broadway's *Rock of Ages* and *Sweet Charity* and *Peter Pan* and *Beauty and the Beast* and *Victor/Victoria* and *Sunday in the Park with George!* Whew!) played Cervantes. The director and choreographer of *Man of La Mancha* was David Wasson, who spent thirty years as an actor and appeared on Broadway in *La Mancha* many, many times. He has appeared on Broadway with Will Smith, Cybil Shepard, Richard Kiley, John Cullum, Robert Goulet, John Raitt, and Harve Presnell. So, ladies and gentlemen of the audience of this show, a testimony to Stutler and

Funking, aren't you amazed that in calendar years 2017, 2016, 2015 (so far, going backward) that in this new millennium, the Westchester Broadway Theatre keeps producing exceptional shows with exceptional talent? Not to repeat myself, as I am apt to do, isn't it *exceptional* of the quality that this unique theatre, under the stewardship of Stutler and Funking, can still produce in this first year of Donald Trump's presidency?

Whew!

Let me quote a unique reviewer, for *Man of La Mancha*:

> "*It's not madness of Stutler and Funking to continue to provide Westchesterites with the best of theatre (Note the "re" on theatre.) It's not madness to ask Michael Bottari and Ronald Case to design a set that dwarfs many Broadway productions. It's not madness to create an environment that succors its audience so well—that I forgot where I was while I was watching the show! Maybe that's the madness of WBT's productions!*
>
> *I seriously don't know where WBT gets such actors as Paul Schoeffler (as Cervantes/Don Quixote/Quijana); Michelle Dawson (as Aldonza/Dulcinea); Gary Marachek (as Sancho, the squire). I could name Ian Knauer, Alan M-L Wager, Geoff Belliston, Joanne Borts, David Cantor, and Joseph Torello and other supporting cast members with the superlatives of theatre that are bandied about, such as "mesmerizing!" or "fantastic!" or "extraordinary singing" or "unbelievable acting."*
>
> "*I can add to the adjectives for Schoeffler—who not only inhabits Cervantes; masquerades as Quixote; and realizes the truth as Quiana—but commands the stage as a knight errant. I could tell you that the lilting, extraordinary voice of Dawson is wonderful. I could laud the pantomiming horses and other theatrical stunts you find on this thrust stage.*
>
> "*I must seriously laud the director/choreographer David Wasson, who turns the thrust stage of WBT into the Inquisition prison. It is in this prison that Cervantes*

gets to act out his book about Don Quixote—with the help of the prisoners, who take parts.

"What a genius of presentation by writer Dale Wasserman, lyricist Joe Darion and composer Mitch Leigh—and the aforementioned David Wasson. I was totally lost in the production of "Man of LaMancha"—I found myself transported to the 1600s. It takes a masterful director to produce such a play."

Then:

OLIVER!
WESTCHESTER BROADWAY THEATRE
THROUGH SEPTEMBER 8, 2013
GARY CHATTMAN

Charles Dickens: It was the best of times, it was the bestest of times.

John Fanelli: Sir, you have that wrong!

Charles Dickens: Who are you, sir?

John Fanelli: I am the director of "Oliver," currently at the Westchester Broadway Theatre through September 8, 2013. And that quote from your book "A Tale of Two Cities" is incorrect.

Dickens: I wasn't referring to my book. I was referring to your splendid production of "Oliver"!

Fanelli: Why, thank you, sir!

Dickens: I found it inspiring!

Fanelli: What particularly did you like about it, sir?

Dickens: "There is nothing in the world so irresistibly contagious as laughter and good humor." I wrote that in "A Christmas Carol." The whole show is wonderful! Carrie Silvernail's choreography is phenomenal! Kurt Kelley's musical direction is tremendous! Steve Lofus designed sets that are unique! Zounds! And you, sir, the Artistic Director

and Producer, is " . . . the last dream of my soul."
That's from "Tale of Two Cities"!

Fanelli: I know. You know, I worked with a wonderful
cast!

Dickens: Of course I know! Did you think I was dead
or something?

Fanelli: Sorry.

Dickens: Where should I start? I will start at the
beginning, of course. That "Oliver," Brandon
Singel, is probably a fifty-year-old midget!

Fanelli: He is not. He is young.

Dickens: What an actor! What stage presence! What a
voice!

Fanelli: Yup, I agree.

Dickens: Fagin, played by John Anthony Lopez, is the
joint!

Fanelli: Huh?

Dickens: Ooops! That's a 2013 word! He has " . . .
is a wisdom of the head, and there is a wisdom of
the heart." That's him. A consummate professional
who takes the stage like Tevye takes the stage in
"Fiddler." A mesmerizing actor.

Fanelli: Oh, you've seen "Fiddler"?

Dickens: Many times. I'm going to go on with my
praise. It is my book "Oliver Twist" that was
adapted for this show, wasn't it?

Fanelli: Yup.

Dickens: I knew it! Kudos for Lucy Braid, who plays
Nancy; Brian Krinsky, who plays Bill Sykes . . .
and an ensemble cast of kids that rivals that of the
Broadway "Annie"! "To a young heart everything
is fun."

Fanelli: Thank you. Coming from you, that is abject
praise!

Dickens: Zounds! I can't praise this production
enough! The powers that be at this dinner theatre

should just turn over their yearly program to you! You are the best!

Fanelli: Again, I thank you.

Dickens: I would like to compliment you, your staff, your cast. This is one of the best shows I have ever seen in Elmsford.

Fanelli: Thank you once again.

Dickens: I had the roast beef for dinner. Did you know that the price of your ticket covers both dinner and the show? And there's free parking, too?

Fanelli: Of course I knew!

Dickens: Sorry. I figured you did. "Happiness is a gift, and the trick is not to expect it, but to delight in it when it comes."

Fanelli: I agree.

Dickens: This show "Oliver" at the Westchester Broadway Theatre is, as the song says, in "Reviewing the Situation" I "Consider Myself" a fan. I just might take my friends Tolkien and Tolstoy to the show next week. I wish to see it again!

Fanelli: You are a gentleman.

Dickens: I can't understand why people would go to Broadway to see "Annie" or "Matilda" when young actors appear on stage at WBT who are their equals or better in talent!

Fanelli: I agree.

Dickens: In closing, sir, may I say, "It is a far, far better thing that I do, than I have ever done; it is a far, far better rest that I go to than I have ever known." I mean, to see your wonderful production of "Oliver" at the Westchester Broadway Theatre!

Fanelli: It's been a pleasure meeting you, Mr. Dickens.

Dickens: For me, too, Mr. Fanelli. God Speed.

For every production, I write a review for:

GARY CHATTMAN, PUBLISHER/CRITIC

SHOWBOAT
WESTCHESTER BROADWAY THEATRE
September 24-November 29, 2015; December 30, 2015-January 31, 2016
October 2, 2015

GARY CHATTMAN, PUBLISHER/CRITIC
SHOWBOAT
WESTCHESTER BROADWAY THEATRE

September 24-November 29, 2015;
December 30, 2015-January 31, 2016
October 2, 2015

Well, they've done it again! What, you ask? What is that special undertaking that Mr. Stutler and Mr. Funking have brought to Westchester? Why, it's the SHOWBOAT! "Life upon the Wicked Stage ain't ever what a girl supposes. Stage door Johnny's outraging over you with gems and roses. When you let a fella hold your hand which means an extra beer or sandwich, everybody whispers, Ain't her life a world . . . "This life upon the wicked Westchester Broadway Theatre stage ain't what you could suppose it would be—for this is Westchester, not Broadway! But here in Elmsford, the SHOWBOAT has docked and it is everything—all gems and roses! I vow: this is the best show ever at an Evening Dinner Theatre/Westchester Broadway Theatre. The best.

The original novel by Edna Ferber was written in 1926. It told the lives of three generations of musical performers on the Cotton Blossom, a floating theater. In 1927 Jerome Kern and Oscar Hammerstein II adapted the novel into a very successful musical that has been revived many times. It was the first Broadway musical to integrate songs with plot! There are two major stories—Julie Dozier and husband Steve Baker, stars of the SHOWBOAT, are accused of miscegenation in racist Mississippi. Magnolia, daughter of Captain Andy Hawks and wife Parthy, is a talented young lady who aspires to the stage. She meets Gaylord Ravenal, a riverboat gambler . . . and that, ladies and gentlemen, is the essence of a hint of the plot—all played out to song and dance and much more on this very wicked Westchester Broadway Theatre stage!

Let's take the principals in this musical extravaganza: There's the ingénue, Magnolia, played by Bonnie Fraser. Ms. Fraser is a lyrical soprano with a vulnerability that gives us, the audience, empathy. There's the riverboat gambler, Gaylord Ravenal, played by John Preator. Mr. Preator is the perfect epitome of a n'er-do-well; his voice and acting mirror the excellence of Ms. Fraser. What can I say about Joe, played by Michael James Leslie? Visit the Playbill *to see this man's credits! His singing (according to my wife) sounds like a reincarnation of Al Jolson. Electricity here! Joe's wife, Queenie, played with verve by Inga Ballard, has a resume befit a diva.*

"He's Just My Bill" sings Sarah Hanlon, as Julie . . . she played Mary Magdalene in a tour of "Jesus Christ,

Superstar"—and she evokes empathy and pathos in her performance. Her stage mate, Steve, is played by Eric Briarley—naturally, with his talent, from the "Les Mis" tour. Jamie Ross is Captain Andy—played with the exact amount of pathos and empathy a father should have.

There's the song-and-dance duo Ellie and Frank, portrayed by Amanda Pulcini and Daniel Scott Walton. Laughter, laughter, laughter. Fun, fun, fun. Talent, talent, talent. And don't forget the snappy Parthy, embodied by Karen Murphy. Her website is www.torchgoddess. com for good reason.

The real kudos for this production belong to the director/choreographer Richard Stafford. The man is a genius! How to make a thrust stage appear like a proscenium one is no problem for this stage genius! Give him a yearly contract and let him direct and choreograph every WBT show. This Stafford WBT SHOWBOAT is superior to the two revivals my wife and I saw in New York. Honest.

The sets and costume design by Michael Bottari and Ron Case (a team for over 46 years) have been nominated for many, many awards. See this SHOWBOAT and you'll understand why. Without the space found on Broadway stages, they have created magic.

Ryan Edward Wise did the music direction and the old stalwart Andrew Gmoser did the lighting. Exceptional work, gentlemen.

I didn't mention all the members of the ensemble . . . yet . . . Karen Webb, Roger Preston Smith, Adam Richardson, Amanda Pulcini, Kristyn Pope, Gabriella Perez, Zoie Morris, Leisa Mather, Paul-Jordan Jansen, Celeste Hudson, Justin R.G. Holcomb, Alia Hodge, Jonathan Freeland, Michael Dauer, Erin Chupinsky, Eric Briarley, Malcolm Armwood—all terrific. I hope I didn't leave anyone out.

So, you have it: My review of WBT's incomparable SHOWBOAT. I could go on and on . . . and on with my raves. This show was so good, my wife and I actually will return to see it again!

Go! "Make Believe" you have revisited a superior musical based on a superior book and you are there. "Ol Man River" passes before you . . . "After the Ball" (show) is over, you will marvel at what brilliant creative minds can produce—even in Westchester Broadway.— only 25 minutes from Broadway!

#

What reviews! What plays! What a theatre! What producers! As Jane Bergere, the Broadway producer, has said, and I requote: "You have to have a love of theatre and also be savvy in business." She said something like that! And you must realize that both partners here, Stutler and Funking (and of course, Von Ann) have continued to present to the Westchester and environs audiences quality theatre in a quality, family theatre of families. You probably ask why I keep repeating myself. I myself am amazed that a business—yes, a business—even one including dinner, musical show, and parking—can continue to exist since 1974 (to today, 2017) for forty-three years. I am amazed that in all my interviewing, not *one* person has had anything negative to say about Stutler or Funking. And the one common denominator, a certain word, comes up from most of the people I have spoken to. That word is *family*. WBT is a family.

That's why I keep mentioning it. I'm amazed, and I'm sure so are you!

Erin McCracken starred in *Always, Patsy Cline*. She had also appeared in WBT's *Hairspray* and in many regional theatres. She also is currently the girlfriend of Ryan Stutler. (Name seem familiar?)

That *Show Boat* that I reviewed (September 2015–January 2016) featured loads of Broadway talent. I know, I know, Stutler and Funking *always* featured Broadway talent. My bad. In that show were Jamie Ross as Captain Andy, from *Beauty and the Beast; 1776; Gypsy; La Cage* and many others. Amanda Pulcini

(Ellie May) comes from Broadway's *Lend Me a Tenor* and *Fiddler on the Roof.* Michael James Leslie (Joe) was on Broadway in the revival of *Hair; The Wiz;* and *Little Shop of Horrors.* Pardon me if I again defer to the exceptional reviewer from *The Westchester Arts and Education Review:*

Backwards in High Heels: The Ginger Rogers musical, ran from August to September 2015.

Uniqueness. As Pia Haas said in the *Playbill*: "*Backwards in High Heels* was conceived and developed by Lynette Barkley and Christopher McGovern . . . It features vintage movie musical numbers as well as original songs to showcase the major events in Ginger Rogers's life." Darien Crago played Ginger Rogers. She has the steps, the voice, the acting. I won't bore you by quoting that noted reviewer again. Just know that Ms. Crago comes from *42nd Street* on Broadway, with Karen Ziemba. To again quote Pia Haas's introduction, quoting Jeremy Benton (director, choreographer and Fred Astaire), "I couldn't be prouder of these eight actors, especially my rising star of a leading lady, Darien Crago. She, like Ginger, has so much talent to give. Audiences will walk away feeling they've witnessed the emergence of a new theatre star!" Jeremy played Bob Hope in the Off-Broadway *Cagney,* as well as having appeared in Broadway's *42nd Street.* Why am I mentioning this? This book is a salute to Stutler and Funking, isn't it? I mention these actors, these plays, to highlight the caliber of this family theatre. I wish to provide you with a list of talent that either has started here or paused here and then gone on to bigger and better things in the musical theatre. That's why. And it's all to do with Funking and Stutler. Yes, the talent, the shows, the ambiance, the food, *the whole business*—the success—is due to Stutler and Funking.

"Midnight, not a sound from the pavement. Has the moon lost her memory? She is smiling all alone . . . let the memory live again." *Cats*: Andrew Lloyd Webber

Memory: 2015: *West Side Story, Godspell, Camelot*. Allison Thomas Lee from Broadway's *The Addams Family* and *In the Heights.* (WSS) Xander Chauncey from WBT's *Jekyll and Hyde* (*Godspell*). Jennifer Hope Wills (*Camelot*) from Broadway's *The Phantom of the Opera.* Look over some of these names, ladies and gentlemen, and when you look back years from now, you may find such successes that are comparable to Kathleen Marshall, Holland Taylor, Kurt Peterson, and Scott Bakula.

Memory: 2014: *It Happened One Xmas Eve; South Pacific; The Wizard of Oz; Mary Poppins; Ragtime; Titanic.* Stars like George Dvorsky (Broadway's star in *The Scarlet Pimpernel*, as Emile de Becque); Haley Swindal (as Nellie, from Broadway's *Jekyll and Hyde*); Bill Dietrich (as Luther Billis, from Broadway's *Sweeney Todd* and *Les Miserables*); *Mary Poppins* flew over the Westchester Broadway Theatre's audience! Lauren Blackman played Mary. She played the part many times previously in regional theatre, and has appeared as Irene Molloy in *Hello, Dolly*, with Sally Struthers. Mary was again directed and choreographed by Richard Stafford.

From time to time the producers brought in shows under the helm of John Fanelli. One show was *Ragtime*, another was *The Wizard of Oz.* Mr. Fanelli said about Bob and Bill, "They gave me my start. They are wonderful people; they gave me the chance to develop." Mr. Fanelli established a network of theatre programs for young people all around the world. In 2004 he developed the Westchester Broadway Theatre's Young Artists of the WBT. He once was the artistic director the Times Square Group of NYC, where he developed and implemented educational theatre programs. In 2006 he founded the Lighthouse Youth Theatre program in Westchester.

"I was lucky. George Puello was the man in Westchester theatre for thirty years. George gets me in there, and they're at first not interested. Then they were. The first show we did was *Les Mis.* Bill thought it would be a kids' show . . . then he was, like, amazed! I was very happy that he liked it. After I left on my own, I told him that the Westchester Broadway Theatre was very important for Westchester County—the apex. The best. I offered to work with them anytime. I was lucky enough to work right alongside them. *Ragtime* sold out. Last time I did *Godspell* for them. It was great fun.

"I'm the kids' theatre guy! Family Theatre Company was to involve kids in my program, Non-Equity, for professionals in Westchester."

Richard Stafford has been a director for the producers for many years.

"Westchester Broadway Theatre holds a very special place in my heart. I moved to New York directly from London, where I had been studying for two years at the London Academy of Music and Dramatic Arts. I am originally from Chattanooga, Tennessee.

"The year was 1979, and my first break was being cast as a Non-Equity dancer/singer at An Evening Dinner Theatre. The production was *The Unsinkable Molly Brown* and I felt so lucky to be in the ensemble for that show. I met some great people— Broadway professionals and newcomers like myself. The show closed early, sadly, but I was then offered *Hello Dolly!* starring the legendary Dorothy Collins. Broadway actor Doug Carfrae was playing Cornelius Hackle and was ultimately replaced by Richard Caspar when Doug left for another project. Richard went on to direct and choreograph many shows for Bill and Bob. I played Ambrose Kemper and sang and danced in the ensemble. I was in heaven. I also got my Equity card on that show.

"I went on to perform on Broadway and in First National Tour and regional productions. I began to direct and choreograph in 1985.

"Years later (2002), Bill Stutler asked me to direct and choreograph *Cats* for the, now named, Westchester Broadway Theatre. I had performed in the show on Broadway and had ultimately became the dance supervisor. Since 2002, I have directed and choreographed sixteen musicals at WBT and am looking forward to number seventeen in the fall of 2017. Needless to say, I learned a tremendous amount about my craft while working at WBT, and I am always welcomed back and feel very much a part of the WBT family. Bill Stutler continues to inspire me in the casting of each show. He is dedicated to actors and can spot new talent a mile away. Four of the shows I have directed have been holiday shows. Bob Funking oversees those productions and has always been incredibly helpful in making sure the productions shine. Lisa Tiso is such an insightful producer—fair, thoughtful, and with a wicked sense of humor. Bill and Bob really know their audience, and what an amazing track record they have. It is such an honor to be a part of the WBT family."

"Once upon a dream, I was lost in love's embrace. There I found a perfect place, once upon a dream."
*Jekyll and Hyde***: Leslie Bricusse and Frank Wildhorn**

SCENE EIGHT:
... WITH ONE PERSON,
ONE VERY SPECIAL PERSON

As you have seen, there have been many special people who have passed through the gates of Westchester Broadway Theatre—have become family—and are now working there. Some have moved on.

Pia Haas, the public relations director, was a student at Valhalla High School. I won't mention the year—women are touchy about their age. "There was a teacher at Westchester Community College named Mark Clark. He would take young actors and actress to different festivals. He was president of the International Amateur Theatre Association. I knew him. He had been approached by the producers about theatre. 'Do you have any kids who might be interested in working here?' Obviously, in 1974, motivated students became motivated waiters, waitresses, hostesses, backstage helpers. It was fun, an exciting new venture. I had a short stint as a server; worked with props, costumes; as a dresser; booths, lighting, sound, stage manager for special shows on Monday and Tuesday nights; designing lights for special shows. I was entrenched!

"I did this all as I went to Sarah Lawrence College; I divided my time between college and An Evening Dinner Theatre. Then I left for graduate school at New York University.

"From time to time, both Bob and Bill called me in as a consultant. For the show *Nine* I was actually the Italian consultant! I taught the cast how to speak Italian correctly!

"We kept up the relationship. In 2008, Bill called me. He said, 'Bob and I don't know what you're doing, but we have an opening for a PR director? Are you interested?'

"Well . . . I was. I spent two weeks with Alan Gruet, who taught me the ropes.

Gary D. Chattman

"I have had a relationship with Bill and Bob for many years
. . . I have always found them very supportive. If I have a question or problem, I can go directly to them. They are definitely
very bright, very knowledgeable about what works and what
doesn't, after all these years of experience . . .

"We have weekly staff meetings to talk about lots of things,
day-to-day running, future season, problems that come up.

"I do enjoy the work. Promoting this theatre and its family
is a daily responsibility. Everyone who works here has a human
and personal interest. That's one reason I keep our blog interesting. It's harder and harder to keep in touch with the public.

"This is a unique institution in this county. It is very special
. . . people have been there a long time . . . family, many grew
up here and know each other intimately.

"I am definitely part of the clan."

Let's hear from Mr. Randy Skinner: "Today I am a director/
choreographer preparing a big revival of *42nd Street* in London's West End at the Drury Lane Theatre. I also teach.

"I first met Bill and Bob when I was hired to direct and
choreograph *42nd Street* at the Westchester Broadway Theatre. I
was immediately taken with the love and care that they put into
the production, doing everything they could to give me what
was needed for a first-rate show. They know their audiences
so well and deliver such wonderful entertainment, which is the
reason they are still in operation after all of these years. That
is not an easy task, to keep coming up with titles that will sell
tickets. Ten years later they wanted to do *42nd Street* again, and
I immediately signed on. *White Christmas* followed in 2013,
and I was pleased to have a third opportunity to work for Bill
and Bob. They had waited many years to obtain the rights to that
show, and their patience certainly paid off for us all.

"The lesson that keeps occurring to me whenever I have
worked at Westchester Broadway Theatre is that if you have a
great show and a talented cast, you do not need a lot of bells
and whistles to achieve a great product. With the stage being
a very deep thrust, with the audience surrounding three sides,
your set pieces need to be thought over very carefully. I loved

the challenge of doing these two very big shows and having to rethink them for a thrust stage. In other words, how do I deliver a big Broadway show in a smaller venue without losing all of the glamour and energy that goes along with musicals like *42nd Street* and *White Christmas*? I am happy to say that we were able to achieve that with Bill and Bob guiding the way."

Amazing, isn't it, to get such testimonials in a business? But this business has been around for forty-three years and counting. And, like I have said many times, it's *family* business with *family*.

Take Bob Arnold. I don't mean literally, "Take Bob Arnold." Listen to what he says about WBT: "I had known friends who had worked at this Equity theatre that did *long* runs and was forty-five minutes from Midtown Manhattan along the Saw Mill/Henry Hudson. There were two producers who loved theatre and always got properties that were audience-pleasers. The production team was top-notch and casts were full of Broadway performers (and those of Broadway quality), but mostly it was because of the brilliant/crazy director/performer/wunderkind Richard Casper. He and the team turned out stunning productions in a room with no fly space, no wing space—in an industrial park. That was An Evening Dinner Theatre.

"It all worked, and everyone wanted to work there! I auditioned for a couple of things, to no reply, and then *Can-Can* came around, and I booked Boris Adzenidzenadze, and they must have liked me because over the next decades I did *ten* different long-run productions for Bill and Bob. They are bosses, friends, pals, confidants, professionals, and I miss working at An Evening as well as Westchester Broadway Theater!

"Did I mention the lifelong associations with friends and colleagues in the business? It's a roster of great maestros, costumers, set designers, staff and crew—and peach melbas!"

Didja know that Andrew Gmoser has been the lighting designer for all of the productions of the producers since 1980. Over the years, he has created sets/lighting for many, many productions throughout Westchester. You can bet that Andrew has a love of lighting design for all theatre levels, from high school through professional Broadway-caliber productions. I remember him from the Asbury Summer Theatre (near where my mother lived in Yonkers) where he worked for thirty years. He has also worked for twenty-two years with the Mac-Hadyn Theatre in upstate New York. He has his own company, Silent G Productions, for which he provides theatrical lighting design, equipment, and theatre, dance, and concert consultation.

Kristen Blodgette, a musical director *parfaitement* is now busy. I have tried calling her many times, but she has an important job. You see, she is the musical director today for a certain Andrew Lloyd Webber fella. She began her career working for the noted producers Bill Stutler and Bob Funking. In the *Playbill* for the current Webber show, of which she is musical director, *Sunset Boulevard,* with Glenn Close, it says the following:

"Kristen Blodgette has been associated with "The Phantom of the Opera" since its New York opening, supervising the Broadway production; the U.S. national tours and companies in Hamburg, Switzerland, Belgium, Copenhagen, Stuttgart, Madrid and Mexico City.

"Additional credits include: "The Woman in White"; "Chitty Chitty Bang Bang"; "Cats"; (Broadway and North American tours, Mexico and Copenhagen), "Sunset Boulevard" (Broadway, Los Angeles and touring production), "Bounce" (Goodman Theatre, Kennedy Center), "Jesus Christ Superstar", (Broadway and Mexico) and national tours of "On Your Toes", "Jerry's Girls" and "Barnum." Kristen is currently the associate conductor of "Mary Poppins" on Broadway. She is presently working on the development of a new musical called "Prairie" with Rachel Portman, Beth Henley and Francesca Zambello."

No wonder she doesn't answer her phone!

SCENE NINE:
THE BEST OF TIMES IS NOW

*T*itanic; White Christmas; Kiss Me, Kate! (again!) Oliver; The Sound of Music; Guys and Dolls; In the Heights; Fiddler; Miracle on 34th Street; Can-Can; The Music Man; George M!; Hairspray; Legally Blonde; 'S Wonderful; Big River; Home for the Holidays; My Fair Lady; Altar Boys; Seussical; Singin' in the Rain; I Do, I Do; A Sleepy Hollow Christmas Carol; Jekyll and Hyde (again!); Rent; Peter Pan; Sugar; Nine; Christmas Voyager; 42nd Street; I Love You, You're Perfect, Now Change; Funny Girl; Meshuggah-Nuns; A Wonderful Life; The Producers; Beauty and the Beast; Buddy; A Christmas Carol; Phantom (again!): Little Shop of Horrors; Gypsy; Grease; Nunsensations; The Christmas Inn; The Full Monty; Hot Mikado; Barnum; Aida; Are We There Yet?; It Happened One Christmas Eve; Gentlemen Prefer Blondes; Anything Goes; Oliver! (again!); Bye, Bye Birdie; Meet Me in St. Louis; Cabaret: And The World Goes Round; Miss Saigon; Footloose; Miracle on 34th Street; Swing!; Smokey Joe's Café; Singin' in the Rain; Chicago; Christmas in New York; Kiss Me, Kate (don't ask); Nunsense 2; Cats; Jesus Christ Superstar; A Wonderful Life; Jekyll and Hyde; High Society; Hello, Dolly!; A Country Christmas Carol; Crazy For You; The Sound of Music; Grease; It Happened One Christmas Eve; The King and I.

There. I've done it. The past seventeen years of theatre at the Westchester Broadway Theatre. From the new millennium till now: a total of eighty shows. Imagine! Eighty shows! How did Stutler and Funking produce *so many shows* for Westchester, New York, and its environs? They must be geniuses! They must have such business acumen! It behooves me to sit back and marvel. What producers in America—ever—have produced eighty shows in seventeen years? Can you name even one? I can't. I can name two: Bill Stutler and Bob Funking.

I could inundate you with the histories of each and every show; tell you the minutiae of every cast member; I could print the reviews from that exceptional reviewer from the *Westchester Arts and Education Review*. It would be a chore, but it could be done. But—wait a minute! I figured that for your enjoyment at this show—the story of the producers, Von Ann Stutler, Bill Stutler and Bob Funking, it would be best to portray this scene with highlights of the past seventeen years! So, here goes!

Glory Crampton starred in *Can-Can* with Tony Lawson, Thenardier in Broadway's *Les Miserables*. *George M!* (their 175th show) starred John Scherer as the lead. He starred in the Broadway *By Jeeves*, as well as worked with Hal Prince on projects. Jim Walton, who played Jerry Cohan, is a noted star on Broadway. Shows include *Merrily We Roll Along; 42nd Street; The Music Man* revival (my wife and I saw him there!); and *Bye, Bye, Birdie*. In that same *George* cast was Laura Schutter, who has been performing on Broadway in *Mary Poppins.*

Broadway's Lauri Landry and Mark Zuckerman (twelve Broadway shows between them) appeared in *I Do, I Do.* Xander Chauncey (of many Off-Broadway ventures and *The Full Monty* with Elaine Stritch) costarred with WBT favorite Michelle Dawson in *Jekyll and Hyde*. This particular show was directed by previous *Jekyll/Hyde* Robert Cuccioli.

Have you heard lately of a revival of Broadway stalwart *Rent* anywhere? Well, in Elmsford, it was revived in 2010. I'm sure you saw it there. So many, many, many people did. I'm sure you remember Andy Kelso, as Mark Cohen, in it! (*Kinky Boots, Mamma Mia*). It is indeed a puzzlement why, in these hard financial times, such a unique theatre continues to thrive. There was nary a seat to be had at the performance I attended, and (!) there was a standing ovation at the end of the show! Why?

I'll tell you. Patricia Wilcox (director/choreographer) brings us these "Seasons of Love" in a free-flowing, ensemble-driven, movement-oriented way. She is a theatrical genius! And she has Christopher McGovern (who I watched carefully during the performance) as her musical director, concentrating on the keyboards and leading his orchestra in the most professional way. And she has Steven Loftus, who designed this set for this thrust-stage production. No wonder he is in such high demand.

Let's discuss this cast. Let's start with the ladies: Steena Hernandez, as Mimi, brought back memories of the original—Daphne Rubin-Vega—only she had more energy, savoir faire, and the empathetic voice that is needed. Mark Ayesh, playing Roger (played originally by Adam Pascal) and Andy Kelso as Mark Cohen (played originally by Anthony Rapp) were exceptional. Sara Ruzicka (in the Idina Menzel part of Maureen) stopped the show literally cold when she sang about that cow that jumped over the moon. I could mention Gabrielle Reid (as Joanne) and Angelo Rios (as Tom Collins) and the many members of this harmonic ensemble as proof . . . proof for what?

That this cast in almost every way was superior to that of any production of *Rent* I have seen!

Nine featured the "couple" of Glory Crampton and Robert Cuccioli. Jill Abromovitz (as I mentioned previously) played Fanny Brice. The show about Funking and Stutler (but this time, producing hit shows that made lots and lots of money, and made lots and lots of people happy, and created a family of performers, staff, and audience in Elmsford) was aptly titled *The Producers*. It was producer Bill Stutler and producer Bob Funking's 158th production. The time: August 2008. Bob Amaral played Max Bialystock (Bob Funking), and Joel Newsome played Leo Bloom (Bill Stutler). Mr. Amaral was in *Lion King, Guys and Dolls, A Funny Thing Happened on the Way to the Forum*, on Broadway. Mr. Newsome was in *42nd Street*. Stutler and Funking starred in Elmsford.

Could'ya believe that Disney's *Beauty and the Beast* actually played Westchester Broadway Theatre? Yup, it did. April 2008. Rena Strober (Cosette in *Les Mis* on Broadway) played Belle, and Joseph Mahowald played the Beast. (On Broadway: *Pirate Queen, Jekyll and Hyde, Les Mis)*. Richard Stafford again directed. Continuing our trip *up* memory lane: Stutler and

157

Funking revisited *Phantom* in 2007, with Kate Rockwell (one of the finalists on NBC's *Grease:* "You're the One That I Want.") and Aaron Ramey (*Zorba* at the York Theatre).

NEWS Westchester Broadway Theatre Will Revive Yeston-Kopit *Phantom* With Ramey and Rockwell
BY ADAM HETRICK
SEP 06, 2007

Kate Rockwell, a finalist from television's *Grease*: "You're the One That I Want," will star as Christine Daae when the Westchester Broadway Theatre revives Maury Yeston and Arthur Kopit's *Phantom*.

Joining Rockwell will be Aaron Ramey (*Thoroughly Modern Millie*) in the title role and Sandy Rosenberg (*The Scarlet Pimpernel*) as Carlotta. Tom Polum, who was a part of the original production and directed the 1996 Westchester revival of *Phantom*, returns to guide Rockwell and Ramey through the gothic musical.

Complete casting and creative team will be announced shortly.

Following the world premiere at Houston's Theater Under the Stars in 1991 starring Robert Cuccioli and Glory Crampton, *Phantom* made its New York premiere at Westchester Broadway Theatre in 1992, running for nine months and spawning the RCA cast recording.

The Kopit/Yeston *Phantom* — based on the Gaston Leroux novel, "The Phantom of the Opera" — predates the Andrew Lloyd Webber version, delving further into the characters' past as well as providing several plot twists not in the original novel.

Preceding the musical's premiere, Kopit's original book was made into a 1990 NBC television miniseries starring Burt Lancaster.

Phantom will run Oct. 4, 2007–Feb. 9, 2008, with a hiatus from Nov. 26–Dec. 26 when Westchester Broadway Theatre will present the holiday classic *A Christmas Carol*. For tickets call (914) 592-2222 or visit www.broadwaytheatre.com.

Audience reactions to *Phantom*: "I have been involved professionally in the theatre for many years now. I witnessed perhaps one of the most breathtaking pieces of theatre I have ever seen. I was amazed by the sets, costumes, breathtaking performances and mind-blowing staging . . . both creatively and technically . . . I am now a very busy hair colorist and have urged all of my clients to book tickets. In the past three days, seven clients have done just that. BRAVO to a job well cone. I have become a season subscriber and I must say that *Phantom* at the WBT put the Lloyd Webber version on Broadway to SHAME!" Gina G., Stamford, Ct.

"What a great show! My group took it in this past Sunday, and, to a person, everyone thoroughly enjoyed the performance. Laughs, tears, frights . . . everything necessary to a great theatre experience was experienced by all. Some of us had also seen Webber's Broadway production, and, of course, there were those who preferred that one, but even those had to admit that WBT's production of *Phantom* was excellent! (And, in my humble opinion, the voices in this cast were far superior to that of the current cast of Webber's production!) Kudos to all involved in the production and extreme compliments to the entire staff (including the waitstaff). As usual—this was not our first visit to WBT—everyone went out of their way to make sure we enjoyed ourselves. And we did!" B. Crane, Brooklyn.

Gypsy, in 2007, starred Karen Mason. Ms. Mason was nominated for best actress for *Mamma Mia* on Broadway; appeared as Norma Desmond in *Sunset Boulevard*; won the Outer Circle Critic's Award for *And the World Goes 'Round.*

Tony Lawson played P.T. *Barnum* in the show of the same name in Stutler and Funking's 146th production. Mr. Lawson also played Thenardier in *Les Miserables* on Broadway. Playing Radames in their production of *Aida* in 2006 was Eric Sciotto, who understudied the role on Broadway and then took it over. Paige Price played Reno Sweeney in *Anything Goes.* She starred on Broadway in the original cast of *Saturday Night Fever.* Robert Bartley, in that same show, played Billy Crocker, after appearing on Broadway in *Miss Saigon* and *Cats. Oliver* had perennial star Michelle Dawson. Dana Moore appeared as Roxie Hart in *Chicago* after a Broadway run in *Fosse, Dancin'* and *Sweet Charity* with Bob Fosse. Her costar in that show was Nancy Lemenager, as Velma Kelly, from Broadway's *Kiss Me, Kate, How to Succeed in Business Without Really Trying* . . . and others. Yes, there were *Cats*—many cats—running around on WBT's stage in 2002. Some of them were Stacia Fernandez (Broadway's *Swing!, The Scarlet Pimpernel, Beauty and the Beast);* Erick Devine (from Broadway's *Ragtime,* among others); Gayle Holsman (from the Broadway show of the same name), and this show, among many others, was directed by Richard Stafford.

Some audience reviews for another incantation of *Jekyll and Hyde*, the Stutler's 123rd production: "Absolutely wonderful!" "It was fantastic!" "Thank you so much for a wonderful evening!" " . . . where else can you get *dinner and a great show* at such a wonderful price?" This time Tom Schmid played the main role (from Broadway's *Annie Get Your Gun*) and (of course) Michelle Dawson. You would have seen someone named Will Swenson in the part during matinees. Currently he is married to Audra McDonald, and a star in his own right. You might remember him in one of the following productions: *Hair, Les Miserables* (Javert), *Priscilla Queen of the Desert, 110 In the Shade,* or *Lestat.*

My distinct apologies to the many, many actors of all of these shows, not only of this new millennium, but of those who appeared on the stages of An Evening Dinner Theatre or Westchester Broadway Theatre: I could not mention all of you! If I were to create this book of 500 pages, I could have and would have mentioned everybody. For their 199 shows, the producers Stutler and Funking have provided their audiences with *professional, Equity casts.* Each and every performer who graced either stage in the past forty-three (yes, forty-three!) years, was a professional. The direction was professional. The meals were prepared professionally. The staff was chosen professionally. But this family encompassed almost 200 shows. Yes, that's 200 shows. *Mamma Mia* in

March of 2017 will be their *200th* show. Do you believe that? It's hard even for me to believe—to sit in awe. So, to mention 200 shows times casts of sometimes twenty-five or more— I would have to mention some 5,000 performers! Really! 5,000 performers! So, again, my apologies. We all know that all members of every cast appear nationwide (and sometimes worldwide) in various professional productions. Many of the Stutler and Funking's cast members have gone on to Broadway or the movies! Imagine that!

The Producers

August - November 08
Book by Mel Brooks and Thomas Meehan.
Music and Lyrics by Mel Brooks. Musical Direction
by Leo P. Carusone, Choreographed by
Matthew J. Vargo, Directed by David Edwards.
Starring Bob Amaral and Joel Newsome.

Based on the 1968 film, Mel Brooks's musical *The Producers* is a laugh-out-loud, outrageous, crowd-pleasing farce that has been a smash hit since its 2001 debut. Fading Broadway producer Max Bialystock is desperate to get to the top of his profession again, and he finds an unlikely ally in mousy accountant Leo Bloom, who hypothesizes that one could make far more money with a flop of a show than with a hit. Together, the two set out to produce the worst musical ever to hit Broadway, with the worst script, the worst director, and the worst cast they can find; the catch is that they will raise two million dollars to finance the show, and they plan to take the money and head to Rio when the show inevitably closes after just one performance. Too bad for Bialystock & Bloom that, against all odds, the show is a total hit! With dozens of big and bit parts alike, no shortage of show-stopping musical numbers, and Brooks' signature humor keeping audiences in stitches, *The Producers* is definitely far from a flop.

Gary D. Chattman

**The Producers, Bill Stutler and Bob Funking.
Address: WESTCHESTER BROADWAY THEATRE,
Elmsford, New York. They care.**

**Note: SPECIAL FREE PERFORMANCE FOR
LOCAL CHILDREN'S HOMES: WEDNESDAY
MATINEE, JANUARY 11, 2017—1:00 P.M.**

*For the past 42 years, Westchester Broadway The-
atre has donated a matinee performance of one of its
mainstage productions each year to the children resid-
ing in the area institutions in Westchester County. This
year the children will be treated to our new musical
production of SATURDAY NIGHT FEVER. This year's
invites include: Andrus Children's Center, Cardinal
McClosky Home, Edenwald Center, Green Chimneys,
Hawthorne Cedar Knolls, Lincoln Hall, Putnam Associated Resource Center, Pleasantville Cottage School,
Pleasantville Short and Gateways, Rockland Children's
Psychiatric Center, Sunshine Children's Home and Tod-*

dlers Park Headstart. There will be over 400 children and chaperones attending this performance. Approximately 16,900 children and chaperones have attended since the program began.

Each of the homes is contacted by a staff member of the theatre, and a need of the institution is met by the donation of gifts which are presented at the end of the performance. Proceeds for the gift donations come from our generous audiences during the holiday season. These gifts include: computers, tablets, color printers, digital cameras, video cameras, TVs, DVD players, microwaves, stereo systems, video games, and so on.

Funds also raised this year for Lustgarten Foundation, Pancreatic Cancer Research, Americares, the Foster House, The Thommie Walsh Education Fund, National Multiple Sclerosis Society, TRR Warrior Camp, Changing Leads, AHAI, and Westchester Homeless.
Re: Pia Haas, director of Press and Public Relations.

County Executive Andrew Spano issued this proclamation on April 5, 1999, but it could be just as relevant for each year, leading up to now:

As Westchester County Executive, I would like to propose a theatre in our county for special recognition by the Tony Awards. This theatre is the longest continuously running Equity theatre in the history of New York State, operating 52 weeks a year. The Westchester Broadway Theatre is located in Elmsford, NY, just 25 miles from Broadway.

On July 9th, 1999, the theatre will celebrate its 25th anniversary. To date, they have produced 114 musicals and plays, all cast in New York City with Broadway performers and creative artists. I am proud to note that Bill Stutler and Bob Funking, the founders and producers of Westchester Broadway Theatre, have produced more musical theatre than many Broadway producers.

163

Over the years, the Westchester Broadway Theatre has been continually praised for the high quality of its productions. In its 25-year history, the Westchester Broadway Theatre has brought Broadway musicals and plays to the residents of Westchester County and the surrounding areas, many of whom have never been to New York City. Busloads of patrons arrive from Connecticut, Massachusetts, Rhode Island, Pennsylvania, and as far away as Ontario, Canada.

Their full-house matinees on Wednesdays and Thursdays have been a cultural home for seniors, schools, and the various hospitals in the area. Their children's shows on Saturdays have introduced many to the magic of live theatre. During the summer, specially priced Wednesday night performances have introduced children to classic musicals. Each holiday season, since the theatre first opened, children from 8 to 10 institutions have been invited, free of charge, to see the current musical production. At that time, each institution is provided with gifts such as TVs, stereos, computers and VCRS.

The Westchester Broadway Theatre has been the starting place for many of today's Broadway Tony Award winners, as well as a home for established Broadway performers when they are performing on the Great White Way.

In the last 15 years, there has not been a musical on Broadway that did not have at least one singer/dancer/actor who has appeared at the Westchester Broadway Theatre.

The theatre provides employment for 175 people. It is a "for profit" theatre which has never solicited from any government or corporate source. After 25 years, I believe, as I hope you do, that they deserve special recognition by the theatre community.

So . . . you see . . .

"To days of inspiration, playin' hooky, makin' somethin' outta nothin. The need to express, to communicate, To go against the grain, going insane, going mad." 'La Vie Boheme': *Rent,* **Jonathan Larson**

Ah, memories. *High Society* had Kurt Peterson; Will Swenson came here, married, a couple of kids, from the Midwest. Bill had to fight with Bob to hire him. Then he was nominated for his appearance on Broadway for the *Hair* revival! As I note within this tome, Mr. Swenson, also married to an actress with four Tonys named Audra McDonald, is an actor today.

You can see that what the Stutlers and Bob Funking created is a real-life "It's really A Wonderful Life." The producers wanted Richard Stafford, who did *Cats* everywhere. They called him; he was a dance captain on Broadway. His brother was serving in Vietnam; John Tesh (then at CBS) came to the theatre to interview him.

Down through the years . . . "There is a fifth dimension beyond that which is known to man. It is a dimension as vast as space and as timeless as infinity. It is the middle ground between light and shadow, between science and superstition, and it lies between the pit of man's fears, and the summit of his knowledge. This is the dimension of imagination. It is an area which we call . . . *The Twilight Zone.*" Rod Serling

Bill Nolte starred as Tevye in *Fiddler on the Roof.* He also played Tony at the Goodspeed Opera House in East Haddam, Connecticut, in the show, *The Most Happy Fella.* "I auditioned for the Westchester Broadway Theatre; I was called in by my agent. I have known the director Richard Stafford since we worked on *Cats* on Broadway. I played the part of Old Deuteronomy off and on for five years; I took the first national tour . . . it was the first big major first job for me.

"I loved working there—it was only a twenty-minute commute to my apartment in Inwood, no traffic, no subway, etc.

"I liked the people, the theatre, the ambiance. Pia Haas is a Facebook friend; she is the only one from there I keep in touch with. They were all very supportive . . . just nothing but supportive. Bill even came to Goodspeed to see me!

"I've asked them to do *The Most Happy Fella* there, but today audiences are simpler when they don't have to deal with emotions . . . they like Disney; it's easier to digest. It's a shame.

"I just finished the last six months of 2016 as Tevye . . . as Fagin . . . at the Cape Playhouse, at the Pioneer Theatre Salt Lake City. I'll be in *Mary Poppins* at the Paper Mill Playhouse in June 2017."

From a review:

God: Well, Tevye, what mischief are you up to now?

Tevye: I'm appearing in *Fiddler on the Roof* at the Westchester Broadway Theatre.

God: You?

Tevye: Well, actually Bill Nolte is playing me. And a superb job it is!

God: Please explain.

Tevye: Dear God, you made many, many poor people . . .

God: Yes, I know. Tell me about Bill Nolte.

Tevye: Bill Nolte is the consummate Tevye. He's understanding, he's boisterous, he's bellowing, he's maudlin. And he has a fine singing voice! He dominates this 177th production at the Westchester Broadway Theatre. His skills are wonderful, for he doesn't borrow mannerisms from Tevyes I have seen in the past. He's just like Harvey Fierstein—but with a good voice!

In an interview, Bill Stutler's remembrances . . . Westchester Broadway Theatre throughout the years: "*Aida*: January 2066, Patty Wilcox directed *Motown* on Broadway; for *Barnum*, Ray Roderick played Tom Thumb . . . now he's directing professionally! For our *Grease*, Karen Mason went to Broadway in *Mamma Mia*. For *Buddy Holly*, that show really built an audience! It was that popular! If you see *Cagney* Off-Broadway, you'll find Jeremy Benton—and alumnus from *Singing in the Rain* in April of 2011. We are really lucky with actors, directors, musicians—they all keep coming back here! *Sound of Music* (June 2013) Michelle Dawson! Meg Bussert auditioned . . . Karen Murphy, who was known as a comic, came in to audition. What an incredible voice! She has been at the Met!

"Zack Tremmer of *West Side Story*—what a voice! I remember *Godspell.* It didn't sell here like it should have. Xander (the lead) and all the Broadway cast took an off night from the show and all of the cast members did a show on 72nd Street! Wonderful! Ah, Happy Days! The seniors who saw it jumped up and down!

As Bill says, "We treat people nicely in case they want to return and in case we ask them to return."

"Only twenty-five minutes from Broadway, think of the changes it brings; for the short time it takes, what a diff'rence it makes, in the ways of people and things." *GEORGE M!* **George M. Cohan**

BOWS!

Before we bring out Bob Funking and Bill Stutler, we'd like to thank our cast.

That is you! You love theatre! You love music! You love eating! Put them all together, and you have: The Westchester Broadway Theatre! And you, as I, as my wife, love going to the family Westchester Broadway Theatre of family!

When you visit Westchester Broadway Theatre, take a look at all the plaques—the awards—that Funking and Stutler have deservedly received.

Marie Spruck and her husband, Steve, have been aficionados for many years: "We are retired (and loving it). We always try to book our shows around our birthdays and anniversaries. It makes for a very nice, enjoyable day out. We have been attending the WBT since it opened. I remember going to holiday shows with our children, and now they are attending with their children!"

And . . . Wayne J. Keeley and Stephanie C. Lyons-Keeley, "grew up in Yonkers and have attended shows here since the very beginning when it was in the first location. I remember seeing countless plays here with leisure suits and buffets!"

And . . . Jeffrey Schlotman (Dr.): "Back in the late seventies I was hired as the understudy to Harold Hill in *The Music Man*. I was also a dentist. They gave me my Equity card after a week. The lead took a television show, and I played Harold from that point on, eight shows a week for months. Now I am the dentist for Bill, Bob, Van Ann, and their families!"

And Allen and Helen Gantz: "We have been long-time members of the WBT. Both of our daughters worked here. We have had the privilege of being the exclusive dry cleaners for the theatre. We enjoy seeing all the new shows and being the caretakers for all the great costumes. Everyone here is not only a team player but a family player!"

And Irene Wallace: "I have been coming to WBT since I have been a child. My parents had a subscription since the inception of An Evening Dinner Theatre. I still remember Chinese food being served for *South Pacific*! This was when I was young. Each time I come here I feel that my parents are still here with me, at the theatre. They are deceased, but always loved it here as well as I do."

And Audrey Pomeranz: "I have been enjoying the Westchester Broadway Theatre since it was a buffet. I took my daughter and parents to see *Camelot* for her sixteenth birthday. When I recently saw it playing again, tears came to my eyes. I come from a family of theatre people with a dad who entertained seventy years and a mom and aunt who played as children professionally. My daughter does opera, and three of my granddaughters are in theatre as well. They love coming here and enjoying your shows. Thanks for all of those pleasant evenings of fun. I always go home, singing and dancing.

"I hope to be around to take my great-grandchildren here as I am sure they will love you as much as I do."

And Paula Wilson: "My husband brought me here today 'cause it has such sweet memories for me, because I used to come with my mom before she passed from cancer."

And Gary Chattman: "My wife and I have been coming here since 1974, one year after my daughter Alissa was born. Throughout the years, I have collected 143 programs—yes, 143 programs—from shows we've seen. When my son Jon was born in 1976, he didn't know then, but he would also be visiting the Stutler and Funking theatres in Elmsford."

* * *

What can I say? I am simply amazed that whoever I spoke to for this tome only had wonderful things to say. The word that was most used was 'family.' You see, Stutler and Funking have succeeded in making their business a family. And I don't throw that word around lightly. All who worked here, from the lowly busboy to the assistant to the director, all call this theatre

169

in Elmsford a family. That's because all were treated with care and respect. And, in turn, treated the producers the same way.

Bob and Bill obviously had great acumen, to take whatever knowledge (and in the beginning it was green) and turn it into such a successful theatre. As I have mentioned, they have produced more shows in the past forty-three years than most producers have produced in their lifetimes—and did it successfully and entertainingly. And even though we are in Trump's America, though they made money, they still showed care and interest in those who worked in their theatres. They made their theatres, not only a place for families to go to, but for that family feeling of those who were the workers. And that is unique in America.

The food served here is of the highest caliber; no grilled cheese sandwiches or franks and beans. No. We have fish; we have a dish for vegetarians, and there is their crowning achievement: roast beef. And there are corn muffins. And there is peach melba. There is caring for even their dessert!

And the productions! Amazing! Amazing! Read the letter from the prior county executive. Each and every one is carefully cast, carefully choreographed and directed. And the result is amazing! And highly professional!

Throughout the years, they have had the benefit of working with many talented individuals—who they let shine. They have been blessed with actors of the highest caliber; directors of the highest caliber. To repeat what Bill has said, "There isn't a show on Broadway today that doesn't have an alumnus from here." And it's true. Many have gone on to superior heights. And they all got their start here, or they stopped here, or they learned here. Many of the aforementioned celebrities have learned their craft here—or earned a living here. How many of you audience members awaken each weekday morning looking forward to going to your job? Hands?

It has been an honor to be a patron of these theatres and to be a chronicler of the lives of Bill and Bob and Von Ann.

* * *

One family member said about this production enterprise, "We keep it together as a family . . . the hardest part is we don't know what is going to happen. Bob is eight-three, my dad is seventy-eight. This theatre keeps them young. They are just like a married couple. Each has a bad ear . . . on a plane they couldn't hear each other. They are always arguing. They share a dual office, share responsibilities: Bob takes care of specials, financials, and my father does the shows. They always know where their stuff lies and what they are good at.

"Their creed is 'I can do that,' and they got that by watching other producers.

"I knew I wasn't going to get far in theatre . . . I needed money outside theatre . . . so, I got into the electrical union. I worked backstage at the theatre. In *West Side Story* in Mahopac, I even played Anybodys!

"This theatre is an unbelievable accomplishment. I got to grow up where people treated me like a celebrity. Till this day, people come up to me! Even when I grew up in Croton, people knew who I was.

"My parents did a lot and enjoyed what they did and do. They gave us a wonderful life, except for the tragedy. We didn't think anything could go wrong. Why should it? I feel that life has to go on. You have to continue."

And now, ladies and gentlemen, the stars of our show: the producers of An Evening Dinner Theatre and the Westchester Broadway Theatre—a family within a family, Mr. Bob Funking, Von Ann Stutler and Bill Stutler!

"Isn't it warm, isn't it rosy, Side by side by side . . . Ports in a storm, comfy and cozy, side by side by side . . . Ev'ry thing shines, how sweet, Side by side by side . . ." *Company*: **Stephen Sondheim**

"We can do it! We can do it! We can make a million bucks!" *The Producers*: **Mel Brooks and Thomas Meehan**

"Give my regards to Broadway, remember me to Herald Square; Tell all the gang at Forty-Second Street that I will soon be there. Whisper of how I'm yearning to mingle with the old-time throng; Give my regards to old Broadway and say that I'll be there, e're long." *George M!* George M. Cohan

EPILOGUE

It is the pandemic of 2020–2021. The earth has moved from under our feet. We mask before we set foot outside in the street. We socially distance. Luckily, in 2021, we have replaced our criminal, unintelligent, uncaring president with the complete opposite, President Biden, who is facing many horrible situations about the state of our wounded country.

We cannot go to the movies. Theatres are shut down. Broadway is closed. And the Westchester Broadway Theatre has closed its doors—forever. It will be a factory. As it shuts its doors and the proscenium curtain comes down for the final time, we remember the past years and the contributions of Bill and Von Ann Stutler and Bob Funking to our cultural history. We remember the oh so many professional shows—mainly musical—that graced the stages of their two theatres. We remember the performances. We remember the scenery. We remember the actors. We remember our visits to celebrate our personal lives. We remember the food—particularly the roast beef. We remember. We will try not to forget, for we carry memories of the Westchester Broadway Theatre in our souls.

The pandemic has destroyed this cultural icon, along with causing the many, many deaths around our country—all because of a virus—the deadly virus that has killed over 300,000 people as I write. This evil coronavirus. This evil coronavirus that has killed so many people—so many Americans—has also brought the curtain down on the most unique musical theatre venture in United States history—the Westchester Broadway Theatre!

It is Christmastime 2020. Usually my wife and I would be looking forward to the many individual performances from the WBT stage for the holiday, as well as their special holiday show. Then would come the announcement of the 2021 season, with unique musicals presented with old-time favorites. For charity,

173

during December, a fifty-fifty lottery of would be held. Fifty percent of the money collected would go to the person, and fifty percent would go toward a charity that WBT supported for children in need.

Not this year. The curtain has finally come down on An Evening Dinner Theatre and its successor, the Westchester Broadway Theatre.

> **"I miss the music. I miss the song. Since she's not with me. It comes out wrong. It doesn't matter how hard I try. I've lost the music. I don't know why." Kander and Ebb from *Curtains*.**

> **"You come in off the street, through the doors of the theatre. You sit down. The lights go down and the curtain goes up. And you're in another world." Robert Caro**

> **"The most beautiful moments always seemed to accelerate and slip beyond one's grasp just when you want to hold onto them for as long as possible." E.A. Bucchianeri**

> **"There's a place for us, a wonderful place for us, a place for us—somewhere. Hold my hand and we're halfway there. Take my hand and I'll show you where.**
> **Somehow**
> **Someday**
> **Somewhere."**
> ***West Side Story*, Bernstein and Sondheim**

Goodbye, Westchester Broadway Theatre. We will miss you—dearly.

Review Requested:
We'd like to know if you enjoyed the book. Please consider leaving a review on the platform from which you purchased the book.

CPSIA information can be obtained
at www.ICGtesting.com
Printed in the USA
BVHW091102220221
600778BV00007B/530